About the Author

Aurora Queens first decided to become a writer in high school. She had an event where she had to keep a group of young children entertained. At the time, she told a simple story that she made up on the spot. The group of children wanted to come back to hear the ending. It was supposed to be a one-day trip that became weekly volunteer work for a year. She loved the smiles that appeared on their faces. It is her dream that her books will take another person to a different world and make them happy.

Dark Ruling: Mafia Queen Rising

Aurora Queens

Dark Ruling: Mafia Queen Rising

Olympia Publishers
London

www.olympiapublishers.com
OLYMPIA PAPERBACK EDITION

Copyright © Aurora Queens 2024

The right of Aurora Queens to be identified as author of
this work has been asserted in accordance with sections 77 and 78 of
the Copyright, Designs and Patents Act 1988.

All Rights Reserved

No reproduction, copy or transmission of this publication
may be made without written permission.
No paragraph of this publication may be reproduced,
copied or transmitted save with the written permission of the publisher,
or in accordance with the provisions
of the Copyright Act 1956 (as amended).

Any person who commits any unauthorized act in relation to
this publication may be liable to criminal
prosecution and civil claims for damage.

A CIP catalogue record for this title is
available from the British Library.

ISBN: 978-1-80439-582-0

This is a work of fiction.
Names, characters, places and incidents originate from the writer's
imagination. Any resemblance to actual persons, living or dead, is
purely coincidental.

First Published in 2024

Olympia Publishers
Tallis House
2 Tallis Street
London
EC4Y 0AB

Printed in Great Britain

Dedication

I dedicate this book to my grandmother, Katherine Marie Sims. May her memory and soul always be with me on my journey. I love you. You will never be forgotten.

Acknowledgments

I would like to thank Jasmine Grigsby, my cousin and the first reader of my books. I would like to thank Greg Gilyard, my mentor, who was there to point me in the right direction whenever I needed a second opinion.

To my loving grandmother, who gave me strength to be the creative person that I am.

To my cousin Jasmine, who was beside me every moment as I edited my book.

To my mentor, Greg Gilyard, who encouraged me to make this book a reality.

Lastly, to the singers, songs, and songwriters who inspired each chapter of my book.

Guide

Campris Wars, 2061-2069

During these years, the world was at constant war using the latest radioactive bombs. However, this became their downfall during a massive worldwide meteor shower. As thirteen countries set off these bombs, they mixed with the meteor and merged with human DNA that created the gifted. Afterwards, the United States was divided into small and large territories owned by crime lords, drug lords, mafia men, and mobsters.

Powers

Sigyeil – A being with an Active ability, marked by a pentagon on their body.

True Seer – Foresees the future and can read auras.

Shadow Marked – Someone who is gifted.

Boomer – Uses sound waves to attack

Tamer – Has a separate animal form that is an active part of their life. Dual communication with their animal form. Can command any type of sifter. If given over to another before death, the animal form may live without their tied master.

Raider – Able to heal the dead back to life or able to command a living person or thing to their death.

Death's Raider – Has both abilities that a raider could.

Medium – Able to communicate with souls. Those who have not passed over, are in induced sleep, a coma or even one with the ability of astral projection.

Astral Projection – A projected picture form of how a person sees themselves in spirit. They can use this form to astral walk.

House of Dane
Kyzari Language: The Huntz

Je ta mi – Well met

De wel a yo mo [De wei ah ye mo] – With love may we meet in the sunrise.

Wu shi er tao [Woo shi er to] – I love you

Min quay e las [Min gway e las] – My heart goes with your soul

Deseark – Descendent

Catholic Titles
Tiers of Religion

Mother of the Sky – Mother Mary

Heavenly Lord – Jesus, Son of God

High Lord – God

Stormy Clouds

Song Dedications: 'Enemiez' by Keke Palmer

May 3034
Bossier City, Louisiana

It was supposed to be an ordinary day. Most mornings, Rhia got up at five a.m. in order to have her food stand ready for the 6.30 a.m. morning workers' breakfast for Colt Engineering Company. However, as she French braided her thick, black locks, she couldn't help but feel that today wasn't going to be the same as others. Her hunter-green eyes flickered gray for only a second. In her family, the ones given the sight all had green eyes. Gray, she learned, was similar to storm clouds. The bright day she could have had was now overshadowed by clouds. Trouble would follow behind her today. Waiting for the right moment to strike. Rhia tried not to think of that as she left her small apartment complex. It was already warming up, and it was barely six a.m. The thick humid feel of an oncoming storm. She was happy that she'd put on her wavy blue skirt and white, cotton short-sleeve shirt. The funny thing about the shirt were its the gold printed letters: DANGEROUS. If you were to ask anyone from her old block, they would tell you Rhia Rivers was so far from dangerous that planets separated the word from her personality. Still, that was what they would say, as they didn't truly know her. If only she had known the changes that would be made this day.

"Hey, Rhia, got here early?" Jack the manager asked as he walked to her food stand. Jack was a fifty-two-year-old male with light brown hair and light blue eyes. He was two hundred and sixty-eight pounds with a round pot belly at five-foot-seven feet. Jack had been married to Mary Ann for twenty-seven years and their daughter was turning eighteen this year. He was a proud father. Jack was also the first customer she had when she first started this stand five years ago.

"You know me. I'm an early riser." Jack laughed because he knew Rhia was really a night owl.

"What can I get you, Jack?" Rhia asked the elderly man.

"Egg and cheese burrito and an extra cream twelve oz cup of coffee." As she prepared Jack's breakfast, other workers and food stand owners rolled in.

"Did you hear that one of the big bosses is coming in today?" Ian McNeal said to Jack as he came up. Ian was a twenty-nine-year-old male with caramel skin; a toned, six-foot-four goal-chasing beast. Other workers said he was friendly and fun loving if a little ambitious. For some reason he always put her on edge.

"Which one?" Jack asks.

"Malachi." Rhia froze at Ian's response. She turned to them and handed Jack his breakfast.

"Didn't you say your boss is coming, so why…" she started to stammer out, but Ian laughed at her.

"I said Big Boss, not Boss. I meant one of the Blackstones was coming. Well, in this case, the head of the family. It will be interesting with him around for a few hours." *Hours? The head of the Blackstone Mafia family is going to be in Bossier for a few hours? It is understandable that he would visit the territory he owns, but why stay so long?* "When will he get here?"

Ian looked at her confused. After all, Rhia didn't talk to him.

Ever!

"Gossip says after lunch, but it may be earlier than that." The roll call bell sounded off. That meant fifteen more minutes before the workers must go inside. Jack and Ian left, and therefore she was able to handle the rest of her small entourage of breakfast-eaters. Once the final bell went off, Rhia had to clean up and prepare for the lunch hour. However, her mind kept wandering. Grey eyes. Storm clouds. Trouble. Malachi Blackstone arrival. What could all these puzzles make up when she was standing in the middle of it all?

As her mind wandered and questions floated around, she didn't notice the time that went by. Rhia was brought out of her thoughts by the loud horn of the first lunch shift. Workers came to her stand and wrote out their orders along with their names. Other food stand owners had their own methods when running their businesses. In order to not have her customers fighting over who came first or in case they ordered the same meal, they could claim what was theirs; this was her own method. It was a process that, being a lone worker bee, she needed to have set up. Till this day, she hadn't had any complaints that could risk her contract.

First lunch shift was over and the second would be starting at twelve forty-five. She had exactly one hour to clean her stand and prepare for the next lunch shift. As she was cleaning up, a dark, black Moxac autodrive pulled up near her stand. The Moxac autodrive was first developed in 2976. It benefited the crime families more than it did rich families. That is because it had four hundred and fifty horsepower range, technology that could only be commanded and coded by the owners, and, let's not forget, it was built to sustain against an old-world missile launch. Only two other autodrives came close.

Three men stepped out. Two were obviously bodyguards

with their wide frame. The third, however… the air around him felt like it was being sucked away. Everything just sort of held still as he played around with his gold cuffs. He had a short lift at the top of his head that showed an even blacker color than Rhia's own hair. However, his edges were tinged red. He was six-foot-six at least with chocolate-brown eyes and a light, coco-colored skin. He was in a gray Kandori suit that she last read costed eight thousand for one to be tailored. She was jolted with recognition of who he was. This was Malachi Blackstone. He whispered something to the guard on his left and slowly they walked to her stand.

At that moment, she couldn't describe what she felt. She could only say that this was the moment she knew that the trouble she felt all that morning was finally closing in. Today, if he had gone to another stand, things might have been different. She could have avoided this fate. The thing about fate. Whatever she wills would come to be true. It was because fate played her hand that Rhia's whole life changed. "What do you have that is light and can be easily eaten while walking?" His voice was a low, deep rasp that brought shivers to her.

"Do you mean health-wise or something that you can truly enjoy?" she asked in her quietest voice. His eyes stated that he was amused by her question, but he responded nonetheless.

"How about something that is a little of both?" His lips quirked up in a smirk. Her heart was racing.

"Then I suggested the grilled chicken, lettuce and cheese wrap." He nodded his head in agreement. She made a quick grilled chicken, lettuce and cheese wrap, and as she was handing it to him, she could see a shimmer of light in her left eye's vision. She focused on the light some more and she realized someone had a target directly on him. Without thinking, she shouted alarmingly, "Get down!" She didn't know if it was her words or something he saw in her expression, but he was already down. And there they were. Behind her little food stand with hardly any protection as the world around them was thrown into blazing chaos.

Of course, Rhia didn't know what it meant for an outsider to save the head of the family.

She didn't know that the split second moment where she had saved his life left her with only two choices.

The Blackstone Rule 7: If an outsider that is male saves the head of the family, then he is either brought into the family as a sworn bond brother or killed.

If an outsider that is female saves the head of the family, then the Head of the family must marry her or kill her himself.

Fire Rains

Song Dedication: Dangerous Woman by Sara Ferrell

Tampa, Florida
May 3034

That morning was the beginning of a disaster. Malachi's mother had been asking him as the head of the Blackstone Family to make the decision to move headquarters back to Bossier City, Louisiana. She wanted to respect his father even after his death. However, he didn't believe that going back to his father's birthplace would help the family. Still, to honor his mother, he was heading to Baton Rouge that day. That was the reason he woke with a killer headache. His first thought was who would dare make Louisiana a war zone. Even if the news they received the previous week said that was the case. More chaos happened in Florida, and that was where they were needed. *Why shake things up?* He had chosen his gray Kandori suit to travel today.

Sean and Paul were waiting outside his door for him. Sean and Paul were twin brothers that were as different as night and day. Paul was dark-haired, blue-eyed and five-foot-nine whereas Sean was blond-haired, brown-eyed and six-foot-one. "Let's go. I need to get this over with." Per his mother's request he would check the status of their Louisiana territory. Sean and Paul were aware of his soured mood and did not speak throughout the drive. In truth he was grateful. Since they took the autodrive Moxac, their hands were free. Paul handed Kai his paperwork that he had allowed to get behind. He hardly noticed the time passing or the fact that they had arrived at Colt Engineering Company.

"Boss, we made it," Sean stated. Kai placed the paperwork into his briefcase and left it in the car. It was quiet outside. A few food stands around the perimeter. If he had been taking it seriously, he would have seen it for what it was. The perfect spot for an assassination.

"Let's get something to eat before our representative shows up. What looks good, boys?" Sean looked around for a second and pinpointed the closest one. The female at the stand was more of a child than a woman. She was around five-foot-four inches and at least one hundred and twenty pounds. Long, midnight-blue waves of curls and stormy gray eyes. Small pert breast and hips that a man could grip nicely. She had the potential to be a beautiful woman in the years to come.

"What do you have that is light and can be easily eaten while walking?" He asked while playing with his golden watch.

"Do you mean health-wise or something that you can truly enjoy?" Her voice was as soft as silk. Barely above a whisper.

"How about a little of both?" His heart was pounding through his chest. He was surprised no one could hear how loud it was.

"Then I suggest the grilled chicken, lettuce, and cheese wrap," she said, and her lips quirked up in a slight smile. He nodded his head since words seemed to escape him. He must've been out of the game too long if this child is stirring him up. She cooked up their lunch. As they waited, he couldn't help watching her. Her skin was light like coffee with a high dose of cream added. Her hands were tiny. Every damn thing about her was tiny. He normally went for tall and robust. However, since his father's death nearly a year ago he hadn't tasted or looked at a woman. Yet this child had awakened his appetite more than any other woman from his past. It was when she was handing their lunch that before his eyes the strangest thing happened. Her eyes focus on something just to the right of his head. As her face contorted in concentration, her eyes flicker gray then hunter green and back. Shock came over him and it was like he was looking directly at gray storm clouds. Even with a white flash of lightening.

"Get down!" she shouted with such a booming voice that Sean, Paul, and Kai dropped down obediently and with pure instinct. They were crouched behind her food stand. Kai looked at this little child. It was then that he realized this was no child, for even though he saw fear clouding her dark green eyes, he also saw the fighter beneath. Her eyes were speaking to him. They said that for whoever created this attack, there would be hell to pay. Reaching in his back pocket, he pulled out an Azai 22, an Indian military weapon that was deadly to all that it hit. It didn't shoot bullets but Raven Dust Caplets. Raven Dust was a gas that decayed the body with minutes. And it never missed its fucking targets. Finding their enemies, he and his guards waged a small war. The clicking sound flooded his ears as he aimed and shot at the man across from them. They went down like weasels hiding in the combs. Bastards just weren't worth the damn ammo.

"It's clear, boss," Paul said afterwards. Looking around, although there were no casualties, there were many injured. He realized two things. His mother was right. Bossier City was home. Their Blackstone legacy began here. Therefore, Bossier City had to stand strong in their hands in order to send a message. Someone knew he was coming here and planned an attack to ruin his family's reputation. They wanted the Blackstones to be seen as weak. They wanted a war and got one. The second realization was that the Blackstone law had been enacted.

The Blackstone Law 7: If an outsider that is male saves the head of the family, he must be brought in to become a sworn bond brother or be killed.

If an outsider that is female saves the family head of the family, then he must marry her or kill her himself. Turning to the strange beautiful ch-*woman,* he wondered how the hell he would explain to her she had a life or death decision to make within twenty-four hours.

Fate is a demon that always gets what she wants. Why she chose today to play around was beyond him.

Blackstone Laws

Song Dedication: Us against the world by Christina Milan

12.33 PM
Colt Engineering Company
Baton Rouge, Bossier City

Chaos was all around her. There was blood and the bodies of the injured laying amidst the floor. There was smoke from the flour that had been shot through. Food stands had been overturned or pushed to the side. Rhia could hear the cries of the injured. Everything around seemed like a dream. Someone had really opened fire at work.

"Rhia!" From a distance she heard someone shout her name. Someone amidst this chaos was searching for her. "Rhia!" Their shout was loud and booming to her ears. They sounded at the verge of panic. She turned left and right searching for the face to that voice. Who was searching for her? Who cared enough to look for her? Since her birth when she was left at that orphanage she had never truly been cherished. No one had ever cared enough to panic for her life if something went wrong. She'd mostly always been on her own. Even with her sisters and brothers having her back. She was still alone at the end of the day. "Rhia!" And then she saw him. Everything seemed fine in that moment. "Rhia!" Jack shouted as he searched for her amidst the chaos. Without even thinking, she ran to him. She wrapped her arms around him and held tight. Everything was okay. Jack was okay. She was okay. So, everything would be just fine.

Jack pulled back to get a good look at her. "Not a scratch on you. That's good. You're fine." Jack smiled at her. Jack's smile was always as if he was laughing. However, in that second, his smile was shaking. And his light blue eyes had lost their brightness. Jack for once looked his age, old and wrangled. Jack was that way because he cared for her. "Sol said you warned everyone before the shooting started. Scared several lifelines off me thinking that you hadn't been able to heed your own warning." Jack cared for her. Even if she was given a chance to relive this day and change it, she wouldn't, because she realized that she had someone who would look for her, and that there was someone else in the world that she would care for. A shadow clouded over them. Jack's tan skin tone paled before her eyes. "Mr. Blackstone…" Jack croaked out.

"Jack, long time no see. Can I speak to you for a moment?" Although his words implied that he was not demanding Jack's obedience, to her well-trained ears she heard the command for what it was. Jack nodded his head and followed Mr. Blackstone a few feet away. How did Jack know Malachi Blackstone? Considering the circumstances, only the company should know the face of Malachi Blackstone. Although everyone was aware that he would be coming today, there weren't many who would have recognized him. Was she too panicked this morning to notice Jack reaction to the news this morning?

"She did what?" Jack shouted. The injured had been hurdled out. Everyone left turned to look at Jack. Jack was staring at her. Jack looked as if he had been handed a gun and told to kill an innocent child. If only she knew that child was her. Before she could move to see what was wrong, Jack was coming toward her.

"Rhia, I need you to be absolutely honest with me. When you gave that warning, was it for a specific person or everyone in general?" *What the hell? Did it really matter?*

"Your answer is a matter of life and death." Jack didn't look as if he was joking. He was totally serious. *Oh, Heavens!* Someone could die because of her response.

"The target was Malachi Blackstone, so I was really warning him, but it saved everyone else in the end." Jack closed his eyes and sighed. Her answer... didn't seem to be the one that he was hoping for. Jack grasped her by her shoulders.

"The Blackstone family has a law that says if a female saves the head of family, then she must marry him or be hunted down and killed." Her brain faded out. Her brain seemed to be registering something that Jack said, however she couldn't seem to grasp it.

"Whose life is in danger?" Her own voice didn't even sound like it belonged to her. Her voice sounded like she hadn't had any water in days, or that she had been smoking the last twenty years of her life.

"It means that if you don't agree to marry Malachi Blackstone, they will kill you." Her knees collapsed under her. Jack tried to catch her, but she pushed him away.

"Who the hell are you? You're not Jack. You're not the Jack I know. Jack... Jack wouldn't tell me that I had to marry some *bastard* or be killed. Who hell makes that kind of law?" It was only then that she realized that she was shouting at Jack. Jack who came running after her. Jack who loved her. And then the tears started pouring out. When was the last time she had cried? She remembered it was eight years ago, when she escaped the orphanage.

Malachi Blackstone approached her. "I understand your

rage. You probably don't wish to marry me as much as I don't wish to be tied down. I'll give you twenty-four hours. Meet me at Club Blue Lagoon with an agreement to marriage or to be killed within the next week. Choose your own *fate*."

Choose her own fate. Eight years ago, she chose her own fate when she helped Adriana field the kids out of the orphanage. An orphanage that raised boys to be soldiers and follow orders while girls were raised to be whores to crime lords and mobsters. The world that they were born into wouldn't lift a finger to help them. Later, she found out that Adriana had bombed the church along with the so-called helpers inside. Although she didn't help Adriana kill them, she also did not disagree with Adriana's methods. She chose her fate when she decided to stay in Louisiana rather than go to Texas with the other kids, her siblings. She fought her way through the streets and survived. She lived on her own and started a business that she loved. Eight years ago, she ran away so that she wouldn't be forced to do something against her will. Eight years ago, she escaped being sold to the Blackstone family. And eight years later, fate pulled her strings again. Fate… that wicked woman who will play the keys of piano strings so that every person will always walk the path she had decided for you.

As Rhia watches Malachi Blackstone and his guards walk away, she made herself a promise. She was a survivor, and she would keep her freedom. By all means necessary. So yes, she would marry him, Malachi Blackstone, so that she may continue living. She would be as quiet and obedient as a mouse. And when he let his guard down, she would be free. She would run. She would disappear so that he may not find her. Instead of staying for the next lunch shift, she went back to her apartment to make her arrangements. Fate caged her once and no way was she allowing fate to do it once more.

12.41 PM

The life of Rhia Rivers is circling back. Rhia may think that She, Althea Goddess of Fate, is being cruel, but as the daughter of her heart, Althea would give her the best. Even if Rhia doesn't believe that it is for her own good. Go, Rhia Rivers. Rise to your name. Become the queen you were always meant to be.

Club Blue Lagoon

Song Dedication: Stupid in Love by Jason Derulo

JT Complex Apartments
3rd Level, Room C

This was Rhia's last night in her apartment. Six years of living there, and only then did she realize how sparse her apartment was. The walls with no pictures or paintings hanging. A few stacks of books by the window. Her mattress with the light-yellow quilt laying on it. In the kitchen, a tiny fridge that only had a large container of orange juice, some crackers and cheese in it. The pantry had raspberry chocolate pop tarts and a can of pineapples. There was a plain, no-scent Brinya Bodyworks body wash in her bathroom and a clean, brown towel. Out of her entire apartment, only her closet was the fullest. Clothes styled for old world and new world. Made by Priscilla on second level. She was amazing when it came to design. Ninety-seven percent of Rhia's closet had been designed and created by Priscilla. That included the jewelry, shoes, and make-up.

Since it was Rhia's last night before she had to go him, she wanted to leave with a bang. She searched her closet. Blue Lagoon had all the tech and taste of new world high society, but the colors, the design, and the music was all old world. Looking among her formal old-world style, she saw the first dress she had gotten from Priscilla. She had gone there after hearing Priscilla made clothes cheap. Priscilla was with a client, and the client was very upset with her design. That client refused to pay for the dress and bought something else from her racks. When Rhia saw the dress, she was enchanted. Priscilla and she had several appointments over the next few weeks. She bought lots of items from her. She always paid on time and never complained about Priscilla's designs. Each time Rhia went to her place, she would stare at that dress. Priscilla gave it to her for being a great customer, but she'd never had anywhere she could wear such an elegant and daring dress. That night, she did. The dress had veiled, long sleeves, and touched the floor with a slit that went to her thighs. In the old world, this dress would have costed five hundred at least. In this world, people would probably pay at least thirty thousand even if made by someone from the new world. That was the way that style now worked.

Malachi Blackstone is thinking that she will come to him meek and grateful to be alive. He is wrong. Tonight, Malachi Blackstone, you will see the woman that Rhia can be, and tomorrow she will be gone. Replaced again by someone less bold. She's going to have him on his knees thankful that she had agreed. Let his hell begin.

10.49 PM
Club Blue Lagoon

As she moved past the line, people turn to stare at her. Her curls were free and shone in the moonlight. She had added ruby red lipstick to give her face more color. Her black, three-inch heels made her seem taller. Some stares were hungry. Some were filled with jealousy. A few of those seemed confused at how she could just skip the line. Blue Lagoon was bought by the Blackstone's. Since Malachi said to come here, that meant she had a personal invitation. There was a tall brute standing at the door, at least seven foot with light green eyes and platinum blond hair. Russian. The Campris wars changed many people, but not like the Russians. If you were more than sixty percent Russian, you always ended up over six feet tall green eyed or blond haired. Didn't matter if you were female or male. That made them easier to recognize in the new world.

"I'm going to have to send you to the back. No one skips the line, no matter the reason." His voice sounded rasped and smoky. She imagined he got hit on quite a few times manning these doors.

"Fine, you can tell Malachi that his fiancée wasn't allowed enter on your orders." As she turned to go to the back of the line like he said, he grabbed her wrist.

"Do you mean Malachi Blackstone?" He looked scared to the bone that he may have insulted his boss's woman.

"Yes, tell him Rhia came by, but you denied her entry." When Rhia said her name, recognition crossed his eyes. That told her that Malachi knew her name, and had ensured that his workers were aware she would come searching for him. Suddenly the Russian let go of her and bowed to his waist.

"Forgive me, Miss Rhia, we were told that you would be coming tomorrow. Justin will escort you to Mr. Blackstone in the back office." He stood back to attention and pointed to a man with similar features to himself. *That must be Justin.*

"Your name?" she asked in my soft, light voice.

"Aleksey." On his lips, his name sounded rich and intriguing. She patted his cheek and smiled.

"Your name is beautiful. I'll tell Malachi you were most respectful to me."

And she followed Justin to the man that she would throw in hell. Or so she believed. Maybe even in the beginning she knew the power he would hold over her. Maybe that was why she was planning so hard to fight him. In the end, they would fight beside one another.

11.03 PM
Club Blue Lagoon

Kai was standing in his office at the Blue Lagoon. Upon his arrival hours ago, the first thing he did was make sure the employees knew to watch out for Rhia. Since he only had her name and no picture, that was the best he could do. He was not actually expecting her to make her decision by tonight, so he made them aware that she may come by tomorrow. "Paul, did you find out anything on who may have attacked us today?" Kai had sent Paul scouting after they left Colt Engineering Company. Sean had accompanied him through the rest of their appraisal of Bossier City. There was a lot more to see now that he decided to return headquarters here.

"The Alexander's run Shreveport and Elias Santiago is currently battling Josiah Jang for Blanchard and Alexandria. Between the three of them, two of them must have cut a deal to overthrow us for the territory. Who it is? At the moment the only positive is Alexander." He had to maintain order in Florida for the last five years and now he walked into a war zone. Before Kai could wonder exactly how to approach this war, there was a knock at his door. One of front door guards entered, and behind him was Rhia. Only it was the Rhia he had pictured as a woman. Bold, beautiful, and daring. She waltzed inside his office without his okay. The only skin truly showing was the splint from her thigh to feet. It made her look more tantalizing.

"You wanted me to come to you when I had made up my mind." His body clenched at that low purring voice. *Gods, she's trying to destroy me!* There was no way she would come looking this way without reason. He dismissed everyone else, and it was just the two of them. He poured himself a cup of 2021 scotch and turned his back to her. If he could see past the burning rod in his pants, this would lessen the need to just take her. He needed to have enough restraint to get through this conversation.

"What is your answer?" He felt her as she moved and took a seat on the couch.

"I agree to the marriage. Only I have some conditions I'd like to add. Like a contract." He wanted to laugh. That morning, he had seen a child who had yet to grow into her potential. Right now, he faced a woman who wanted something and was willing to pay the price. He wondered how she would change and grow while married to him.

"What are they?" And as soft as it was, he heard her let out a small sigh. Rhia was still on shaky ground even though she looked confident in herself.

"There is a woman who designs everything I wear. Before I came here, I heard the landlord… let's say demand that she sleep with him or live on the streets. Wherever we may go, I want Priscilla to come too."

That would be easy. If this Priscilla woman had made this dress she adorned now, he was definitely not against her continuing that work. He nodded and she took that as his acceptance. "Jack walks me down the aisle. I don't know what your relationship is with him or whether it is good at the moment. Jack has stood beside me from the beginning. He told me about his family. He watched out from when some the workers tried to give me some trouble. He... he is like the father I always wanted." She didn't stay mad at him long. That was good... maybe she could help bring Jack back into the fold. Jack had saved his father's life forty some years ago and became a sworn brother even at such a young age. He left the organization when Byron, his youngest boy, was kidnapped and later returned to him. That was almost ten years ago. He nodded again in acceptance. "Lastly... we have separate rooms." Quickly, he turned to face her. Her eyes said she knew exactly what she was against. He walked over to her and leaned above her.

"Why? You and I both can feel the sparks. There is chemistry between us. Our marriage doesn't have to be without some great sex." Her face scrunched up like he had said something disgusting or impossible to do.

"I... can't do that stuff. You're asking for too much." It was what she wasn't saying that made things click.

"Rhia, how old are you?" Her eyes flickered pure gold. *How does she do that?*

"Twenty-two." *Twenty-two, Heavenly Lord, she's eleven years younger than me. She truly is a child.*

"And yet you have never been with a man." He was not asking. He was making a statement. Her eyes flickered between gold and black. After a few moments, gold stood steadily.

"No, I never have, and I never wanted to." Before is the unsaid word to his ears. Okay, he can give in now to his virgin bride and show her the art of passion and pleasure later.

"Then we agree on this contract and shall marry next week."

Blackstone Wedding

Song Dedication: Love me Back to Life by Celine Dion

Blue Lagoon
11.27 PM

Maybe Rhia was trying to be too bold. When Malachi said that he agreed, her heart leapt, only to drop when he said the wedding was next week. She knew that she wasn't prepared to marry Malachi, but she thought she would have some time. At least a month. What's the rush?

"You should call me Kai. Those close to me call me Kai, and that includes my wife," he said as he finished the scotch from before.

Gods, am I the only one burning up right now? When he asked if she had been with a man, she really did consider lying just to hurt his pride. In the end, she told the truth. "I do have a question." Really, she had agreed to this farce of marriage, what more was there that he needed to know?

"Why do your eyes change colors?" Shock came over her. Seven years ago, she managed to track her last living family, an aunt. Her mother's sister. She had needed answers and Embry was the only one with them. Of course, Embry met her when she was told she had cancer and only a few months left to live. Embry explained things and told Rhia about her mother. She would never speak of her father unless out of hate. The one with the green eyes holds the power. Their family survived because of their gifts. Only those born or destined to be in their family could see the change. To everyone else they were a steady hunter green. Her mother abandoned her at the order of their family. That ruined them because for some reason there were no more green-eyed babies born, and the others had gotten old and died. What did it mean that Kai could see the changes?

"Depends, sometimes they flicker with my mood. Other times they give warnings. It really depends on the color and how light or dark it is." He handed her some sparkling champagne and sat next to her on the black, suede couch.

"So, what does dark gray, pure gold, and plain black mean?" He saw it all. How didn't she notice that? No, he never reacted oddly, so how could she have noticed?

"Umm... dark gray is a warning for trouble, pure gold means I'm being totally honest and plain black means I'm lying." She answered without thinking of the repercussions. Since he could see the changes, if he knew what they meant, then she wouldn't be able to hide anything from him.

"Do your eyes change all colors and shades?"

"Even some you may not know of." When Kai stared at her intensely, she began to think she may have made one more mistake today. That was agreeing to marry him in order to survive. Although she had grown into a predator by her own right in that moment, through his stare, she didn't think she would ever have the upper hand. Kai would always be the predator in their presence. And she would always feel like prey, even if she didn't show it to someone else.

"It is getting late. I'll get someone to take you home. Once word hits the streets that you are my fiancée, it won't be safe to go out alone. So, the food stand is finished, understood?" This didn't really surprise her.

"I want Aleksey. He's your doorman. He was very kind but firm with me. I want someone like that around me." He took a moment to consider what she had said, and then pressed a button on his desk.

"Sean, bring Aleksey the front guard to my office." There was no reply. Sean, whoever that was, must have instantly obeyed his boss's order. "My mother and sister will be here tomorrow. Circumstances have forced me to make Bossier City headquarters again so they are coming here. My mother can help you with the wedding preparation." Aleksey and the tall blond bodyguard from earlier that day entered the office. *He must be Sean. Better put names and faces together if it will be a while before my escape.*

"Hi, Aleksey. Apparently, you are now my bodyguard." She turned to Kai. "Right, Aleksey, is my new bodyguard?" Kai tensed which told her he was going to switch Aleksey as quickly as possible, but now he couldn't. It would ruin his reputation within his organization.

"Apparently so. Take her straight home." And he tossed Aleksey a set of keys. Rhia didn't sleep a wink that entire night. Within hours, her entire world had been reconstructed.

May 17, 3034
Mary Green Catholic Church
10.15 AM

Rhia was a nervous wreck. In fifteen minutes, she would walk down the aisle and say her vows. In fifteen minutes, she would marry Kai Blackstone. "Stop shaking. Everything is going to be fine," Lucia Blackstone said as she held Rhia's shaking hands. Lucia was Kai's sister. She was twenty-five with his strange hair color and dark, brown eyes. Lucia was chocolate skin-toned and five-foot-nine inches. She was also very kind. In fact, Lucy and Geneva, Kai's mother, were both so kind and sweet. It was hard to place them in the picture Rhia had of the mafia. Geneva was the same height as herself. She had dark brown hair that reached her waist and dark brown eyes. Genny and Lucy had welcomed her with open arms and made this wedding possible. However, at the last minute, here she was choking with nerves. "We have guards everywhere so there is nothing to worry about." She didn't care if anyone crashed this wedding. She really didn't think she could go through with it. Jack stepped into the room, and suddenly she could breathe. Jack had accepted walking her down the aisle. He looked ten years younger in the black Tamor suite. Paid by Kai, it cost at least four thousand.

"You ready?" She took Jack's hand and walked out of her room, following Lucia.

10.31 AM

When the church doors opened and Rhia walked down with Jack, everything else around him faded away. Jack's wife, Mary Ann, wanting to do something for Rhia, had given her her mother's wedding dress that had been passed down through family. It was absolutely gorgeous on her, even if it was old world-styled. That elegance that always seemed to float behind her was in full frontal view.

This woman... she's going to take the world by storm.

He took her hand from Jack and they faced the priest.

"I vow to be honorable and loyal.

I vow to stand beside you...

To always protect you...

I vow to love you with my heart, soul, mind, and body.

Even if Her Heavenly Mother of the Sky should separate us in death.

I vow to love you throughout three lifetimes.

To search and find you in the next life.

To love and protect you until the end of our three life lines.

So decreed by the Mother, watched by the Heavenly Lord and obeyed from the commands of the High Lord."

With their vows, he kissed Rhia. He felt the scorching heat of passion from that first kiss. It was like swallowing the sun. So scorching, yet the need for it makes you return. Their tongues intertwined and their breath stopped. He could feel their hearts beating steadily, cycling and binding them. Becoming one. Rhia pulled away first. Her eyes flickered deep purple with spots of green and shadowed behind mercury silver. Amazing! The crowd shouted with happiness.

Honeymoon at Marakitza

Song Dedication: Start a fire by Ryan Star

Marakitza Hotel
8.13 PM

The change in headquarters and the fact that a war was heading their way meant that Rhia and Kai couldn't go far or be away too long. That's why he had decided to have a three-day honeymoon at Marakitza Hotel. Considering their relationship, it shouldn't have mattered if they went on a honeymoon or not. No one was really expecting one, knowing that this marriage was because of the family laws. That was why Rhia needed this. Kai was giving her a small break before she was thrown completely in. Also, during this time, Kai could give her some key points to watch out for.

 Pulling at his tie to breathe a little, he stared out at the landscape. The sun was setting with a deepening blue. Marakitza catered to the elite high society, which meant those that owned full states. Clothes rustled behind him. "Priscilla, what the hell is in this case that I can wear? This isn't a real marriage, you know." Rhia tried to whisper as she talked to her designer on the communicative phone. "I'm not comfortable with these clothes." She hissed at Priscilla. Curious as to what was in the suitcase, he followed her voice to the bedroom. Clothes were littered everywhere. Nighties, lingerie, and other wisp of clothing that others would have been fine with , but not Rhia. Even if it was lace or sheer veil, he liked that she liked her body to be covered from chest to feet most days. From the looks of it, everything would touch her knees at most. In this heat, that would be better for her, yet she'd kill herself before adorning it. "There better be something in here or you will be sending me a whole new set of clothing tonight." Thrown over the right side of the bedpost, Kai saw a nightgown. It was teal, long-sleeved, and from the shoulder to the top of the thigh was a silk cloth while the thigh to foot was nude veil. Grasping it by his finger, he lifted it up.

"How about this? It will touch the ground, I'm sure." Rhia looked at it and blushed a deep red that he didn't think she could pull off.

"Priscilla, I'm going to kill you!" She hung up. She may have meant that now, but she would probably change her mind later. She forgave the ones that were closer to her. She grabbed the nightgown and slammed the door of the bathroom. Rhia was not yet mature. She was childlike, cheerful, and had a strong head on her shoulders. In the average world she would have been just okay. Here in the crime life, with the right push, whatever it may have been, she would thrive. Everyone started out innocent. Many just following in the footsteps of their father. However, there comes a day when a button is pushed, or a line is crossed. That awakens the person they will become.

Kai's own line was crossed when Lucia was three. He was only eleven and his parents went out to eat. Unaware that some idiot had gotten into his head to start a rebellion, by the time he had made it to Lucia, a guard had a gun to her head. He never thought, but simply reacted, which resulted in that guard's death. Lucia and he had to hide in the safe room with the nanny until reinforcements came.

Rhia was a strong girl who didn't like to show weakness, nor did she understand her own emotions well. However, she had control, and when she bonded with someone it was for life. When her line was crossed there would be many who needed to watch out. Rhia came out of the bathroom, and Kai wanted to thank Priscilla at the same time as kill her. The gown hugged Rhia's figure perfectly. It showed off the woman she was. Made him wish that he hadn't agreed to not touch her. "Don't say anything. Heavens, this is a disaster." She took her tiny hands and ran them through her locks. For some reason it made him smile. Depended on the eye of the beholder, he thought. Her eyes shimmered and he remembered.

"Rhia you said your eyes when they change color represent a warning or emotion right?" Looking at him in confusion, she nodded her head.

"So, what does mercury silver represent?" He could tell she was contemplating being so forward with the information.

"It's not really a warning. Mercury silver is like welcoming the moonlight. A new light. Of course, the person holding the light doesn't always mean they come with good intentions. They are more like guides and the light is a path. They're guiding you down the brighter path even if you must go through darkness to reach it. When did my eyes flicker mercury silver? I was too out of it to pay attention." Tugging at the nude veil with frustration, she was not actually watching him.

"After we kissed. So, what does a strip of dark purple like lightning, zigzagging over your true hunter-green mean?" Rhia stopped and she stood looking at him with shock.

"My eyes didn't change to full color?" she asked and sounded unsteady.

"No, why? Something wrong?"

"My eyes only change to full color. There is no meaning behind what you just described." He understood what had her unsteady. Uncharted territory that no one had explained to her. He walked over to her and took her hands into his own.

"No matter if you understand this, we will work it out together. From this day forward we stand together." Dazed, she agreed. "Let's get some sleep. Tomorrow is a long day."

May 18, 3034
Marakitza Hotel
Private Spa Suite B

Kai said they were getting a massage the second Rhia woke up. She had never had a massage, but she couldn't say she wasn't enjoying herself. Her masseuse, a woman name Karen, knew exactly how to get kinks out. It was so peaceful that she could have been asleep, but Kai was drilling information into her while they got their massages. "In the Blackstone family, there are six people you must be careful around. My cousins Lucien, Maya, Bella, and Dimitri. Their parents Devon and Grace. Uncle Dev always believed that he should have been the head of the family. Although they never do anything physical every last one of them will try their best to make you look like a fool before the family." Her? A fool?

"Why?" She could understand them making her look weak, so why was he saying something different?

"The family knows our circumstances. So, everyone is already expecting you to be weak. At least in their eyes. They will give you time to show your strength. However, stupidity is something else, that can't be seen from the head of the family, and I'm your partner. That would be enough cause to ask me to step down." So, they wanted to play with her. She could be weak, but she was no idiot, nor was she a toy. "Aleksey is never to leave your side outside of our home. War is coming and someone will try to attack you or take you." Yes, but the true question was how this war would end. Maybe only a soldier or fighter could understand that in war, no one wins. Blood will always be shed and lives will be lost. "Leave us," he commanded our masseuses. "Do you know how to use a weapon of any kind?" he asked. *Do I tell him about the first two years I lived on the street? The Blood Rings. No!* "Don't lie to me. Your eyes went plain black. Do you know how to defend yourself?" He demanded of her.

"You forget I lived on the streets. I had to survive somehow," she snapped at him.

"Rhia, just tell me if you can defend your damn self." And if her next answer wasn't the one he wanted to hear, she was in trouble.

"When I first hit the streets, I joined the Blood Rings to make money. They called me Red Wing." And he knew that name, she could tell. Blood Rings' names have meaning. He stood and moved her wavy hair out of the way from her eyes. He kissed her forehead and something fluttered in her heart.

"When the time comes, you *must* kill. Red Wing may have defeated her opponents in there and let them live, but Rhia this is different. You could die." It was only then that she realized their stance. Her sitting on table with only a towel covering her body and Kai standing between her legs. She flushed. The room was heating up.

"Umm… could you step back or something?" Kai smirked and his lips crashed against hers. Last time it was so hot. Like inhaling the sunlight. Now she was drowning without any air.

Gasping, lips being pulled under. She could feel everything about him. His hand twisting into her thick, wavy, long hair. Something thick and hard poking against her stomach. She needed air. And there it was. Kai trialed a kiss against her neck. He sucked between her shoulder blade and her neck. "Wh… what's… what's happening to me?" Her voice was soft and heavy at the same time. Gods, she burned deep within. Kai pulled away.

"I'll take things slow, but that is only a taste of what you could have." He sounded so shaky, and then he left. And damn the man. Whatever he had started why didn't he finish it? Why leave her with such an *ache*?

Homecoming into Hell

Song Dedication: Fighter by Christina Aguilera

May 21, 3034
Blackstone Manor

"This is where we will live?" Rhia wondered if Kai could hear the disbelief in her voice. He told her that they were going home, so she had pictured this five-bedroom, one-story home. This... this was very far from her imagination. It was ten feet high and eight feet wide. Three stories by how the outside looked. Red brick and Sarim rack steel holding it together. Sarim was harder than any other steel, but was a steel not beaten by titanium. Kai didn't look at her as he helped Sean and Paul haul off their bags out of the Moxac autodrive.

"Yes, is there a problem?" he asked. *A problem? Is there a problem?* How about the fact that this place was too big for them, Lucia, and Geneva. Why would they need so much space? She turned to question him what the deal was, but then the door opened, and twelve men came out in black suits, including her new guard, Aleksey. Sean and Paul followed them to the honeymoon, but Kai had said that Aleksey had to stay behind for preparation. They line in two opposite rows and bowed before her and Kai.

"Welcome home, *Don*. Welcome home, *Dona*." Their voices echoed past the street. *Dona*? Umm... she knew she was the only one uncomfortable with this. Kai took it all in stride as he walked through the front door. She had no choice but to follow him. The inside was frightening. So much space, but it was beautiful. Gold and red striped walls, diamond lights, a chandelier in the high middle ceiling. Dark red carpet and a white gold staircase that splits into two leading upstairs. The living room had two wide burgundy couches and a ninety inch flat screen with ivory colored carpets. The kitchen was made for someone who loved to cook. Madeline Brocks appliances everywhere with gray, white, and white gold marbled counters. Persian dark brown table and matching chairs. Madeline Brocks was the new world version of Betty Crocker. She made appliances that allowed the cook to work in a nice environment and when done everything else, the mess leftover, would be absorbed into the deletion component. The component told the cook when it was full so that they could throw away the trash and replace the bag. "Do you like?" While she had walked into the kitchen to get a feel of it, Kai had come up behind her.

"I love it." She really did. There was no reason to lie about that. "How many rooms does this place have?" She was curious. She had only seen the living room and kitchen, but there must have been more.

"There are four rooms and a bathroom on the first floor. Six rooms with their private bath on the second floor. Five more on the third floor. Our rooms are on the second floor. We have the master's room. First and third floor are for the guards doing their rotations. That doesn't include Aleksey, Sean, and Paul. They will be here at all times because they are our personal guards." Something was niggling in the back of her mind. Something he said wasn't right.

He was sitting at the stool by the marble platform. "I bought this house because of the kitchen. It seemed like you would be more welcomed with something like this. My mom and Lucy cook but only on special occasions." He chose perfectly. She cooked for business but that was because she couldn't afford more than that. Living on her own, she learned to curb her habits. When she lived in the orphanage, there were times that she was stressed or simply had to clear her head. Those were the times that she went in the kitchen and played around until she was calm again. Here… she could do that again. She was sure that no one would be against that. "We have a problem… some of my family is here. And the elders are coming tonight." Elders were men who had worked alongside his great grandfather and still lived. They didn't have their hands in the business, but they helped decide what was best for the inner family. In other words, they would decide if she was right to be the *Dona* of the family.

"Which one of your family members came?" His eyes flashed with hate and anger.

"My *Tio* Dev, *Tia* Grace and my cousin Lucien." So, the first day in, and they were already trying to take Kai's seat. Which meant their real target was her.

Blackstone Manor
6.13 PM

She had cooked a feast. She didn't know why she was trying to impress his family. Three elders had come. Jonathan 'Switch' Mitchell was a short man. In fact, she could look him directly in the eye. He was around one hundred and forty in weight yet he looked slim. He had jet black hair and deep night skin. His eyes were wondrous in sky blue. To others he may be considered ugly but she found him beautiful. He was quiet but he seemed to like her, as he said coming in, "To get to a man's heart you must fill his stomach. It smells wonderful whatever you are cooking." She didn't even know how he knew she was the one cooking.

Alejandro De Luz was six foot with jet black hair, and was tanned. He had earth-green eyes and weighed two hundred pounds, yet his wide shoulders made him look more muscular. He was Jonathan's partner... lover... husband. Both men didn't look a day over sixty but that was normal now. Although they aged, their looks would stay the same after a certain point. For many, the age limit is fifty. Even if they lived a hundred and thirty years old, they would look that age, which was their stopping point.

Victor 'Ice' Payne earned his name. He was cold. She would have mistaken him for being Russian if not for the fact that his eyes were gray and that Russians can't wear contacts. So, everything on him was real. The near-white platinum hair and six-foot-five height. Also, he had muscles packed onto him. The elders, Genny, Lucy, Kai, and she had made it to the dinner table at six like she had said it would be. However, they had to wait for Kai's uninvited guest. It was pissing her off that they were purposely making everyone wait as a power play. And yes, it was on purpose. Since she did not wish to disrespect her food and everyone who had come, she was holding that temper of hers on a tight leash. Jonathan looked on the verge of throwing something. Kai said that he got his name because of his temper. Jonathan was the nicest man in the organization until the family was threatened in any way and then his 'Switch' was awakened that left grown men pissing in their pants.

They walked in as if they had not made everyone wait. Devon 'Dev' Blackstone had light brown hair that had red edges.

A family trait, apparently. He was five-nine in height and a hundred and sixty pounds of fat. His eyes were coal black. Other than the hair, she saw no resemblance in him. Grace was six-one in height and a hundred and thirty pounds in weight. Her red brown hair flowed to the middle of her back in loose fashion. Lucien was the exact replica of his father, except that he was six-three in height. That must have brought Dev down a peg or two.

There was no apology for them being late as they took their seat. Rhia clenched her teeth and stared at Kai on her left. There was a small perceivable shake of his head. Now was not the time to move against them, was what he was saying. Grasping her utensils, she dug into her meal that she had spent many hours cooking up, and yet the warmth had escaped it due to their lateness. That was wrong; food should be savored while it is hot. She saw Grace smirk out of the right corner of her eye. *Grace must think they have the upper hand. She couldn't be more wrong.*

"So, Kai..." Grace smoothly cut in as everyone was just beginning to eat. "Did you check to see if your beloved wife was not involved in your assassination attempt?" Rhia was going *to kill* her. This gnat thought she could step into her territory and dismantle her character. "After all, it would be quite foolish to just take her word for it. Someone could be using her to get close to you. Where would the Family be if you allowed someone into the inner circle without first checking them out?" Grace was so confident and sure of herself. The wedding was so fast she must have thought that Kai rushed everything with no suspicions whatsoever. This woman didn't truly know Kai. Everyone must go through a test to understand where their loyalty laid. Everyone takes it even if they are not aware of doing so, just like Grace. Kai understood that they were not loyal to him. He also understood that they would never do anything to harm the organization. That was the only reason that the three of them were sitting there rather than... let's say a more uncomfortable place.

"Her background is very questionable. She is an orphan with no ties and many secrets. I understand if you allowed another part of yourself to do the thinking than your brain." Meaning his dick. Grace was undermining Kai before the Elders. However, she was attacking Rhia. If Kai went after her, his uncle would have the leverage that he needed to take the seat. "You're young, so don't be stupid. Rhia shouldn't be addressed as *Dona* until we are sure that she can truly be the *Dona* without any problems." Something snapped inside of Rhia. Grace was not questioning her loyalty, she was rebelling against Kai's authority. Kai had given her the title *Dona*. She knows that he commanded the men to obey her as if she was him. He stated that she was his other half, so that no matter what happened, she had control if he could not stand. That was his authority. That was his promise to her. From the moment Rhia accepted his proposal of marriage, it would be them against the world. Grace was disavowing his authority before the Elders. She was making him look stupid. She made it seem as if he was weak. Rhia observed her. On the left base of her neck a vein throbbed strongly. It is a good vein. If she struck just right, Grace would die with hardly any blood splatter. Grabbing her steak knife, quickly standing, Rhia placed that knife against Grace's pulsing vein.

"You are an idiot," she whispered in her ear in a deathly soft voice. No one moved. Devon blinked as if he never saw her move. Maybe he didn't. She was Red Wing, after all. Red Wing moved like air. The flutter of a humming bird wings didn't even compare. "In the Blood Rings, you learn that everything and anything is a weapon. Confidence and strength mean nothing. Someone wins by utilizing their brain to find their opponent's weakness and twisting it to become their strength. Red Wing..." Grace sucked in a small ounce of air at the name. "Always defeated her opponent even if she didn't kill them. Even knowing that she wouldn't kill them, her opponent didn't wish to face her because they knew that if Red Wing ever wanted blood their death it would *not* be quick or painless."

She pressed the knife close to her vein. "If you don't learn to obey your leader, you will be the first blood that Red Wing tastes. And I *will* make it as bloody as possible. Choose your own fate." Grace's eyes were glassy with understanding. The Blood Rings was new world version of street fights, except they were legal. They would put two fighters in a pit with various hidden weapons. It was a fight to the death. Red Wing, a fighter that had come out eight years ago, had broken that rule. She would injure her opponents to the point where they had to be hospitalized for weeks. Grace and everyone else now knew that Rhia was Red Wing. And very capable of ensuring her threat. Grace nodded her head in agreement. Rhia sat down and continued her dinner. Dev, Grace, and Lucien seemed scared beyond reason. Death was quick and merciful, but she would leave them alive and in pain. Sitting at the table surrounded by her new family, she knew she couldn't run like she had originally planned. No matter what happened, this was where she was meant to be. *Dona* to the Blackstone Mafia.

Atlantis Sky
7.30 PM

Yes, Althea thought, *my daughter Rhia, make that first step.* Rhia had understood faster than Althea had thought she would. It would not be easy rising to her name. Then again, being Queen is never easy. Daerhae entered Althea chambers. Her dress spun from golden fabric shimmers at Althea's feet. Daerhae was Althea's prophetess. Her eyes that saw what would come to be of Althea's children. Ethan, Althea's son, was lost to her forever. Rhia's foolish family cast her out, believing she would only be their destruction, when in truth she was their salvation. Daerhae had long dark brown waves and pale, white skin. She was over six feet and towered above Althea. Unfortunately, Althea's granddaughter had her genetics to a capital T. Daerhae's dark, night-black eyes shone before Althea. "What do you see? Will she love him? Will she find peace? Tell me if I am doing right by pushing her back onto the path? Is there any happiness in her future?" Maybe Althea shouldn't have asked Daerhae for so much, but she could not stop herself. This was the last of her blood. If Rhia ended, there would be no more of her past. No more essence from her love Vikhtor, her demigod lover that was now trapped in the depths of hell. No possible way to free him.

"Rhia is the flood gates that will awaken a new family. She will love and be loved. She is his light in a book of darkness. Together they will forge a new beginning for all of the lower lands. And bring the key into your hands." Daerhae was telling Althea that with Rhia, Vikhtor may finally become free. *Is the world that has changed so much ready for Gods and Goddesses once more?* Even if it wasn't, none of that would matter. *Rhia, embrace the person you can be. Unlock the doors and free your ancestors. They will atone by always protecting your kin and bloodline.* This Althea swore.

11.19 PM
Blackstone Manor

Tonight, Kai's dear beloved aunt made the wrong move. He thought it would take months before even one of Rhia's lines would be crossed. She had not shown the colors of the woman that he could see past her veil, but she did prove that she was not weak and that she was loyal. He could thank his aunt for crossing that very first line. *Rhia Blackstone, turn this world upside down and show them who the true* Dona *is.*

Crossed Lines

Song Dedication: War of Hearts by Ruelle

Blackstone Manor
May 27, 3034

There comes a moment in everyone's life that shifts everything that they would know and creates a different road for themselves. For most it is their dark troubling past that shifts and changes their future. Especially during the times that they lived in today. One truth is that it is always something unexpected. It is a moment that the person experiencing it can never predict what may occur. As much as Kai would like to say that marrying Rhia changed nothing, he was wrong. Marrying Rhia changed everything. For one, he was slowly falling in love with the woman that he called his wife. And he had been raised to shut off every emotion. Therefore, even as he was falling, he didn't even know that he was. He couldn't stop himself from running into that brick wall. Rhia was his shift. She was changing everything inside of his world and creating her own.

The day they came home she showed dominance and strength by forcing his aunt to step back. The next day she made them leave, and the Elders before they went to their own homes within Bossier City acknowledged her as *Dona*. Since then, she'd been quiet. Not even putting up a fuss when she realized they would indeed be sharing a room and bed. He hadn't touched her, and each night he'd go to bed with a wild fire burning in his blood. However, during training, their true emotions came out. He would admit that Rhia could fight. She wouldn't have survived the Blood Rings without knowing how to fight. The problem was that she refused to kill. Every time he'd point it out, she'd say she wouldn't do it. Today was the same. She flipped him over her shoulder and had the knife pressed dangerously close to his heart. Perfect way to kill. Except…

"This way, in a few slices hitting vital parts that won't kill, my opponent is down in seconds," she stated and behind her, Sean, Paul, and Alek sigh in unison filled with hopelessness. They had come to watch just in case he called them in to switch. Still, Rhia didn't understand the key point. He rolled her off of him and helped her stand.

"Rhia, there will come a time when the choice is out of your hands. It will be your life or someone that you care about, and the only outcome is your death or the death of your enemies." She rolled her eyes and crossed her arms, pushing her perky breasts higher. There wasn't time to acknowledge their attraction. They were at war and a disadvantage. Their enemy knew exactly who they were and where they lived. They had no information on them and that made Kai wary. "Death waits for no one." Rhia's eyes flickered stormy gray and she sucked in a deep breath. Her eyes were glassy and she spoke without really seeing him.

"Carry a weapon on you at all times today. Not a gun, something smaller and thinner. A weapon that would be hard to find on a body." Rhia knew that he always carried a Rystic and Azai, but she was asking for something different. She told him her eyes helped to warn her, but this seemed different. As she left the training room on the first floor, his instincts raced through his core. *Trust her words and prepare for battle*. He didn't need to ask her what stormy gray meant. He already knew the answer thanks to the attempt on his life. Stormy gray meant trouble was coming for them.

3.48 PM
Blackstone Manor, living room

His *madre* followed him into the living room. He had just been informed that there was a ninety percent chance that the one attacking his family was Tariq Alexander. Alexander controlled Shreveport, Texas, and half of California. Still, his home base was Shreveport, which made it understandable to try and move them out of the way. Then he could have a clear path for Alexandria. With a possible lead on their enemy, he wanted his family to be warned. His *madre* had other ideas. She wanted to go *out* during a quiet war. At least it was quiet for now. That could change at any time.

Lucy and Rhia were sitting on the couch. Lucy had on a teal and dark blue dress that reached her thighs. When she twisted around to see them, it changed to sunset red and dark blue stripes with silver stars moving around. However, his very conservative wife, he learned, preferred old world-style clothing. Today she wore a cropped, sleeveless turtleneck that was light blue and a ruffled white skirt that touched her feet. "Kai, I understand that you are the head of the family, but I am your mother and Bridget has called me out of desperation. I must go and see her." His *madre* had that no-nonsense look on her face that he knew he had inherited. In that moment, their looks were identical. Bridget was his mother's younger sister. Bridget got hooked on Essence – a drug that gave off the experience of the perfect orgasm and hadn't been right since. She'd do anything to get the drug, as it was very addictive. Even betray her flesh and blood. Sell her own children if she had any. And his *madre* wanted to go to her when someone had a target on all of their heads. *No way in hell!*

"Not happening. Alexander may be waiting for just that."

His *madre* scoffed and stated, "She's waiting at Brimstone." Brimstone. The house that his father bought for his mother before they were serious. His *madre* was once his father's mistress. He bought Brimstone and kept her hidden there. Till this day, it was the highest, most securely-placed in Bossier City. That meant Bridget was serious when she said she needed help. He closed his eyes. Even though he didn't know his aunt well, she was still family.

"Take five guards with you." Before he could even finish his sentence, she was off commanding the closest guards to follow her. Rhia was searching his face.

"What?" She leaned against the sofa.

"Tariq Alexander. You believe he is the one behind this war?" No, but he couldn't ignore the possibility.

"Doesn't it all seem obvious? Like someone is purposely showing you a set of cards and hiding the winning one." The soft voice was pulling him in. Bewitching him as he stood before her. Her words made him more uneasy.

7.20 PM
Blackstone Manor

Rhia was upstairs in their master bedroom. Only a few days, and she was living a lifestyle that if she had not been forced into, she could have loved. This room was a spice of the old world-style. Egyptian black silk quits with red and gold pillows. There was a table with a mirror. It was egg-white with sky-blue stripes. The perfumes and jewelry stood up at the table. She didn't normally like perfume or jewelry, but Kai chose perfectly for her. Meridians blue teardrop necklace. It was created in 2021 and lost in 2037. How it survived was beyond her, but it was elegantly beautiful. Pyros diamond earrings and anklets. Created in 2043 and handed down through the Pyros legacy. One Rhia thought was extinct, but Kai said that his mother was from that bloodline. A little chair that she could sit on and prepare herself. For what?

Of course, some of his things stood beside hers. His cologne, his watches, and his cufflinks. Everything was black or white. Starring around, it was in these small moments that she wished she wasn't forced to marry him. Maybe she could have been happier if she had freely chosen the man, Kai Blackstone. It no longer mattered. She had made peace with herself and her situation. She wasn't running away. Whatever life she may live by standing beside him, so be it.

A shiver crawled up her back and she grabbed the Azai 22 from under her pillow. Lately, something was awakening in Rhia. She thought her eyes only changed color to give warning, but today while training it was as if she was seeing the future. Men in black masks crashed through the windows. Smoke bombs clouded the view. Racing down the steps to help. Coming face to face with something that she called *death* without a thought. Blood splattered against the walls. She was hoping it was a part of her imagination yet her instincts screamed. Pathways would be changed with this night. She clutched the gun tight in her grip. Lucy and Kai were downstairs waiting for Genny's return. Everyone was so on edge that for once, since she took over the kitchen dinner, it had gone untouched. Clash... the windows shattered. *Rhia, move your damn ass. Protect your family.*

She raced out the room and down the stairs. Destruction was already in the making. The guards were too easily apprehended. At the bottom of the stairs, through the smoke, Rhia searched for Lucy and Kai. She came into the open way of the living room and there was a click near her head.

"Don't move," someone threatened her tightly. As the smoke cleared, she stared into the face of man that she believed long dead. Jason Josiah Jang. The priest from the orphanage. Kai and Lucy, like herself, had a gun pointed to their head. Alek, Sean, and Paul were nowhere to be seen. She didn't think, she simply reacted. Raising her arm and gripping the gun, she pointed at the second man that she recognized had a gun to Lucy's head. Tyler Trenton Jang. They were identical twins, except their auras always allowed her to tell them apart. She only ever saw their auras. Damn good thing, too. Trenton Jang was a pedophile who understood what she could become. Josiah Jang was a cold-blooded killer who never believed she had what it takes to do the extreme. "Rhia Ambria Rivers… been a long time since I've seen you. In fact, the last time we met you allowed your sister to kill my disciples. My children!" He screamed. The Jangs had aged. Dirty blonde waves, dark blue eyes and chocolate skin. Josiah didn't try to pull the gun from her. He knew she would shoot. And neither of the twins liked pain.

"Yeah, I thought you had died right along with them, you monster." She didn't scream, yet her words were not as soft as normal. Kai looked at her with confusion. Her eyes said that once they got out of this, they would have a long talk. She didn't think Josiah would allow that talk. For a cold-blooded killer, he was real mouthy.

Blackstone Manor
7.26 PM

Rhia knew the man that had the gun to her head. How? Her gun was trained on the other man that was identical to the one standing before Kai. He was at fault. Ten minutes earlier, Tariq Alexander called and said that they needed to talk. He didn't sound like a man planning war, so Kai sent Alek, Sean, and Paul to bring Tariq to him. Instead, they were ambushed. He would swear that history was repeating itself from the last time a gun had been at Lucy's head. Except he was sure the outcome would be dangerously different from the last time. "Funny, eight years ago I was planning to sell you to Devon Blackstone. He was growing tired of his wife. And now eight years later I found out that you married the head of the Blackstone family." Rhia's face showed disgust for a split second before everything shifted into a frigid façade. There was nothing in her eyes, in the quirk of her mouth, or the lines of her muscles. It was as if she shut everything off. "I came to kill him, but I think I will take you and the girl. Trent can have some fun with her even though she is not his type. Too old, right Rhia?" She didn't move, but something shimmered in the back of his mind. An echo of her voice.

Touch her and I'll skin you alive only to roast your ass. Rhia was furious.

"And you… you will pay for their deaths. I'll torture you until you are begging for death."

Beg? You will be the one pleading. How the hell could he hear her thoughts?

"Rhia…" Rhia stared at Kai even as she kept the gun trained on Tyler. "Death waits for no one," he reminded her. Earlier that day he had said those words to her. It was to teach her that in this new world, where crime ruled, it was kill or be killed. She nodded at him.

"Anything is a weapon." Those were the words she had told his aunt as she held the steak knife to her neck. Concealed within his arm he pulled out his blade. Swiping at the guy to his side, Kai hit his liver and he dropped. Although he didn't see it, Kai heard her gun go off and he knew it was a kill shot. No time to think, he threw the dagger and lodged it into the man's chest. He went down and Rhia didn't look as she twisted her gun and busted his kneecaps.

Sean and Paul crashed through the door. Lucy was standing, not moving an inch. Kai saw the mess and he knew that they needed help to get it cleaned. Rhia crouched over the man she shot but they had both allowed to live. They needed information and he would give it. "Josiah Jang, you should have died during the bombing. That would have been a merciful death. For threatening my family, you will beg for death. And I will not give it to you. Meet the monster you never *saw*." And Rhia wasn't talking about him, in her ice-cold, hunter-green eyes. The monster that Josiah would face was the one Rhia must have kept on a leash for a very long time. That night, she dropped the chains from that beast inside of her. She stood, took Lucy's hand and walked into the kitchen. Most likely to give her something warm so she would come out of shock.

"Sean, take him to the shack out back. Paul, call for a cleanup. Let it be known that Tariq Alexander is our enemy. He set us up and left my family vulnerable. I'll kill him."

And a third man stepped through Kai's door. One he had never seen before. "I hate that you are very wrong in that aspect. In fact, I may just be your only ally in all of Louisiana." Kai realized that standing before him was Tariq Alexander and that only left more questions. No enemy, no matter how cocky, walks through their opponent's door. What the hell was going on?

Althea certainly was not expecting that. Rhia had called on the Hunter's Clan bloodline and forged a bond with her husband. She forged the Huntzguard bond with him. This would tie them mind, body, and soul. In the last thousand years not one of her descendants had done that even by accident. *Dear Rhia, are you ready for such a bond?*

Weathering the Storm

Song Dedication: Heart by Heart by Demi Lovato

Blackstone Manor

Lucy was going into shock. Rhia didn't think that was possible considering she must have seen this growing up. She decided that her sister-in-law needed a warm cup of hot chocolate. The homemade version. Going to the cabinet, Rhia pulled out a bar of pure chocolate. She saw the blood stain on her hand. That would be hell to get out. "May Lin…" She called out to our system. Every home had a system control. She had never used her before. Too robotic for her taste.

"Yes, *Dona*." The first thing May Lin adapted to was calling Rhia *Dona* and Kai *Don*. It was really weird to hear the house talk back to her.

"Help me… get rid of this stain." She didn't want to startle Lucy by saying blood. Lucy was already too shaken up. The water was scalding hot, and Rhia didn't question whatever May Lin used to get it out, but when it was done the blood stain was gone. Rhia chopped up the chocolate into thin strips. She put them on a slow burn and added milk. Within minutes she had a warm cup of hot chocolate. "Here, drink up." She handed Lucy the cup of chocolate. Lucy sat there holding the cup for a while.

"Has Kai ever told you yet how he made his first kill?" Rhia wasn't expecting her to ask such a question after everything that happened tonight.

"No." Lucy looked up at Rhia and her light blue eyes shimmered with tears.

"I don't remember, but everyone says the guy he killed a man that had a gun to my head." And Lucy had a problem with that. Maybe guilt. "Tonight taught me that I can't sit on the sideline. Can you teach me to fight?" Rhia knew that everyone knew how to wield a weapon, but only Kai seemed to know how to fight. Lucia was done being protected was what she was saying. So Rhia agreed to teach her, and without paying attention to her surroundings she went up to their bedroom. Behind the closed door, Rhia's walls tumble and the cries couldn't be held in. Laying against the bed she cried with all of her soul. She didn't regret killing Trent. She only regretted that it came to one life or another. That in the end Kai was right. Death waits for no one. Death is not a patient mistress. Death takes when the time comes. And Death gives the living the push to the ones whose life line is cut. That night, Death had allowed Rhia to live, but Death took something from her. Rhia wouldn't ever get that piece of herself back. She would live with it for the rest of her life. Strong arms pulled her into a warm chest. Kai didn't say anything as he holds her. Rhia shattered in his arms and she was remade. Kai was the thread putting her back together. Changing her very being.

8.00 PM

Although Kai had not met Tariq Alexander before, he was not picturing this. Six-foot-nine inches full-blooded Native Indian. That earth-red brown skin tone should have screamed

Indian, but it was his long, straight, black hair pulled into a ponytail and dark brown eyes that made it more obvious. Full-blooded Indians, while not extinct, were a rare sight to see. His name made me believe he was of African descendant. His race, like his name and persona, were full of mystery. "What do you want, Alexander? Seeing as you walked through my own door tells me my battle doesn't stand with you." Tariq didn't smile or smirk. Tariq nodded his head and sat on Kai's couch without his permission. Clasping his hands together, he breathed in deeply. *Weight of the world on his shoulders, huh?* Kai had bigger damn problems.

"Only came to tell you there is more at work than a small war. Some outsider is trying to take all of Louisiana. Their main targets are including myself, Francesco, and you." Julian Francesco owned Lafayette. The key pointers. They owned the gold mines of Louisiana. Oil, gas, iron were still in very much in demand. Shreveport had bundles of gas, Bossier routed iron for sixty percent of the Territories and seventy percent of other countries, and Lafayette shipped the oil for all of the United Territories. That was because the city owned the rights. No one else could field out oil without Francesco's okay. Separately owned, it just made good business, under one leadership someone could gain control of the entire the United Territories and a few countries. By the High Lord, now more than ever the three of them needed to work together.

"Judging by your body language, you understand what they want to do. They are already messing with my shipments. I can't be fighting with you while I'm trying to keep my own territory together. That's why I came here. Wasn't expecting to walk into an attack." Didn't matter at the moment. Kai saw that May Lin had already created new glass for the windows. He would have to reprogram her security detail. Alexander stood to leave. From the corner of his eye, Kai saw Rhia going upstairs. She must have calmed Lucia down. Alexander shook Kai's hand. "Francesco and I have agreed to help each other if this person becomes too much." He really didn't like the fact that it may come down to that. Someone wanted to become an emperor. Lines had been drawn and changes would be made. "I did hear that whoever this person was they knew the Blackstone Family well." Tariq's words shook him.

"How well?" If Kai had a traitor amongst them, it was his responsibility to take care of them.

"Enough to know that Blackstone isn't the family name. That is just the name you give others. In today's time, knowing one's true name gives you power over them." The inner family. Their traitor was inside the inner the family. Their true name, Volvikov, was only known to the inner family. He walked Alexander out and went upstairs to check on his wife. Lucia was waiting for *madre* downstairs. The door was closed. Rhia didn't close the door all the way ever. There was always a small crack. Walking inside he heard her. Tears and cries wracked her body. Pain filled his heart. She'd balled herself up and even that wasn't enough. She had a tight grip onto the quilts and they were pulled close to her face. Silencing most her cries, but not all, apparently. He pulled her into his chest. She didn't fight him as she gripped his shirt and continued to cry. He rocked her back and forth. He tried to rub some warmth back into her skin. She was bone cold.

"Nothing is going right." Her voice was scratchy and dry. She hiccupped between her words. She may have been emotionless during everything that happened downstairs, but that didn't mean she was naturally emotionless. Still, it wasn't good for her to cry this much or this hard. Kai forced her to look at him. Her eyes were ghost white with stripes of orange going across. He didn't want to think about what that could mean. And neither should she. He crushed his lips against hers, but at the last second, he softened the kiss. *Forget, love. Drive out your pain and come back to me. Burn with me.* He didn't know if she could hear him through this new bond they shared. He'd try anything to end her pain. He pulled on her lips and pushed her back against the bed. He stroked his hands against her body softly. Across her waist, up to her chest, and down her arm. He wanted her to feel. He wanted to breathe that fire back into her. He held her breast into his hands and he held them firm yet soft. He dragged his lips down to her neck. He trailed kisses above her breast where her heart was.

"Stay here. I'm here. Everything will be fine." He whispered to her. He was actually praying that she will hear him. That she would listen to what he was trying to say. Pushing her shirt and bra down, he sucked her nipple into his mouth and tugged. Swallowing it whole and clamping down tight. "Ahh…" Her voice was soft, rasp, and seductive. To him, her voice always sounded soft and seductive. He tugged at the blue jeans she had put on before dinner. He wanted them off. He kissed her belly button and she jerked. Her skin just a breath away. Her breast rose with each breath. Her skin became darker as lust gave in to the hue of blush.

Good. Don't see or hear anything else. Feel only me. Her jeans came off along with her panties. He spread her legs. She was already coated with honey. He feasted upon her. Rhia pulled at his hair, but he was not stopping. She needed a distraction. As he lapped upon her cream, he could feel the heat build within her body. Boiling in her liquid juices as he sucked on her clit. Slipping his tongue between her folds until she was so wet that drips of her cream escaped him. She burned. The fire taking every thought, sense, and touch. Her hands were tight as they held onto his hair strands. "Stop..." She was pleading yet she pushed her honey closer to him. He stroked her deep within. Rhia was no longer holding him back as he didn't feel her fingers tugging on his hair strands. "I can't..."

Yes you can. And she exploded upon him. Like a bomb going off, her honey poured from her folds and he drank up, filling his tongue with her honey cream's taste. Thick and sweet. He swallowed and drank until the ache began to dull from her. Until she panted with that last breath of ecstasy. Her black waves were spread like the painting of the sun rays. Her dark blue laced shirt was hazardous. One shoulder length was pulled down and her belly was showing. Her eyes were their brilliant hunter green again. He picked her up, folded the quilt down and slid her in. Nicely tucked in and sated, she fell under in seconds.

Gods, this woman; he loved her and he never wanted to lose her. Not even to her own emotions. His *Dona* was awakening into her own person. Until she could piece herself into one full new being, he would be there. To lift her spirits and catch her before she hit the ground. She was more than his wife. She was his heart and soul. He would stand beside her. He kissed the top of her forehead and went to take a shower. They both needed cleaning up, but she needed rest more. Tomorrow... tomorrow was always another battle.

"He loves her already." When Althea has lived thousands of years, she watches beings be born, grow, love, create, destroy, and die. Yet love doesn't work so quickly with mortals. Even though she knew love didn't work that way, Althea knew that he loved her daughter already.

"And she loves him." Daerhae states behind. *Love and happiness is what Althea had always wished for her descendants. None had lived long enough to have that.*

"They will love each other as if their next breath depends on it. When the war is over, love will keep them together. And they will find happiness." *A tear slides down Althea's cheek. She prays that she is right as stone. That nothing will change Rhia's future. Though she is the Goddess of Fate, even she can't control everything. And many will wish to see her daughter fall. Althea prays to the Huntsman Clan. Protect your blood.*

The Mistress of Death

Song Dedication: Silver Lining by Hurts

6.23 AM

The breaking of dawn woke Rhia. Something hot warmed her back. She twisted her head just a little and saw Kai. He had her pulled against his naked chest. She could feel his heartbeat. Last night's memories rushed through her and she flushed a deep red. She should throttle him for going against her wishes, but she enjoyed herself. More importantly, it allowed her to grasp her emotions firmer. And last night they were so connected. She'd swear she heard his voice inside her head. Yet that was impossible. She moved his arm from around her and sat up, and... shit, she didn't have on any panties. It was so odd to be sitting in bed with nothing but a shirt on. The silk quilts cooled her flushed skin like a gentle breeze. Kai shifted and the sheets slid to his waist. He had this amazing tattoo that, even though they have shared this room for a while, she never paid any attention to on his body. Probably because he was usually wide awake and that made her too conscious to stare.

It was a black scorpion with his stinger aimed at his heart sucking in a red chain with a golden key attached to it. She wondered about the meaning behind his tattoo. It was beautiful yet deadly. Like the man himself. He had a six pack with a thin line of black hair going beneath the cover. "Had your fill yet?"

His voice was low and still a little tired. She glanced up and that ache in her body began a low burn.

"Yes." Guess she couldn't hide this time. He smirked and stepped out of bed. He had on blue briefs. It was a first for them both. Then again, after last night, what was the point in hiding any more? He went to her drawer rather than the bathroom. He pulled out black, skinny leg pants and a red V-neck along with her purple push up set of underwear. He handed them to her and went inside of their closest. He was going to wear a business suit today, then. The closet held what she called their image clothes. Those that they wore when trying to make an impression. While he was searching for his own clothes, she ran to the bathroom. Looking in the mirror, she didn't recognize the person there. Red blotches clouded her neck. Her wavy black hair was slightly knotted. This was a woman who had experienced the sun and the moon. The light and the dark. Fire and passion. Last night she caught a taste of that woman. She was afraid of what would happen if she fully gave in and let that woman reign.

She stepped into the shower. The shower and bath were separate. She let the hot water wash over her. She lost herself under the pounding water drips. That was why she didn't hear the door opening and closing. Or notice the slight cool air that come through as Kai entered the shower room. She almost didn't feel the gentle touch of his fingers against her back. She wanted to turn and face him, but he held her in place until she gave in and stood still. With a gentle caress, he roamed the soaked towel against her body. Leaning back against his body, she lets herself go. His touch was the most peaceful she had felt in weeks since all of the changes flowed into her life. She hadn't had time to adjust. He worked his way through her body, from top to bottom, and he was not demanding anything from her. As they finished up their shower, she faced him. Malachi Blackstone. Head of the Blackstone Family. Mafia. *Don*. Her husband. She didn't care that she didn't chose this life. Fate played her hand and brought them together. They were definitely on for a crazy ride and this man was slowly taking over her.

Standing on her tip toes and wrapping her arms around him, she brushed her lips against his. Soft and hesitant, she opened herself up to him. She sucked at his lips and tasted raspberry with chocolate. She pulled on his tongue until he dove in. Thrusting his against her own softly and slowly. Giving her a taste of the powerful force of attraction they had, but not pushing his will onto her. He didn't try to take control of the kiss; he simply accepted what she was willing to give. Light filled her soul and she came alive. She pulled away to breathe. Kai rubbed his knuckles against her cheek. And for the first time in years, she smiled. A blinding brilliant smile. This man... he made her realize how cold and lonely she was before he came. He brought her happiness.

"Get dressed and meet me in the shed. There is someone you wanted to talk to waiting for us." Josiah Jang. She was surprised that he was allowing her to have control of this situation. As she dressed, she decided to wear her hair up. She pulled it into a ponytail and went without jewelry and makeup. It was shocking what the small things do. She'd grown used to being small and feminine. With her hair up and her hunter-green eyes, it made her look like a small predator, but a predator nonetheless. Kai was already in the shed, according to Alek. The Manor echoed with silence. He had sent Lucia and the rest of the guards to Brimstone. It was just them and their personal guards. They passed by the eight-foot-wide, ten-foot-deep pool and the private pool house. Inside the shed, Kai, Sean, and Paul stood to the sides. Josiah was tied to a chair with a bandage around his knee. He didn't look as if he had been harmed since she shot him. He didn't know what he made her unleash. "Hello, Jason." He went crazy. Shaking in his chair. Trying to come at her. Only the chair was nailed to the floor. "You bitch. You think that you'll get something out of me, but you won't." She smiled like a cheshire cat. Yes, she would. She pulled out her Ray-Phaz. It played music, took pictures, and kept time. She scrolled through her music and found Trizha Bowers. Trizha sang electronic dance rock. Most people got into the beat and didn't hear the music. That girl left a message in her music. Rhia decided to play Death Comes Calling. It connected with her feelings. She didn't ask Kai for his blade. She just held her hand out and he gave it over to her. Then she worked Jang over to the message of Trizha.

Death comes knocking on my door. Death, that mistress, calls my name. She says it's time to come on home. They say before we are born we are a flint of stone, the wisp of the wind, a slight in the veil. We do not exist. The High Lord shapes us in his hands. Weather human, animal, or plant. He gives us form and sends us on our way. Allows us to have names. Find memories and live our lives. He sends his disciple death to end it when our time comes. We may have followed the path he chose. We may have not. As the father that shaped us he forgives us. And ask Death to call us back home.

By the time she was done, Jason was a mess. No longer a beautiful elder man. She used the blade to carve deep within his face. Lines etched his chin, the sides of his nose, and beneath his eyes. Dark red blood drips from each etching. "Tell me a name." Rhia demanded. He glared at her and she went for the extreme. Cutting away his pants and grasping his dick in her hands, she held the blade to his tip. The thin flap was ice in her hand.

Shriveled and disgusting. Flabby and weak. He jerked in her hands. "Tell me a name." Jason was sweating and shivering at the same time.

"They call her *Madonna*. That's all I know. I swear." His voice cracked as he gave over the information. He was probably hoping she'd leave him as he was.

"One more thing. Your brother was a pedophile, but you *played* with the girls before you sold them. Right?" He blinked and that was the only answer she needed. She took the blade and slid from bottom to top. Splitting him open. Digging deep and hard as she tore through the muscle to split him open. Jason screamed like the many girls must have as he raped them. *No mercy*. His emasculation was not enough to quell her vengeful desire. As death hardened in her throat, the thirst rose beyond compare. She found his deepest vein and sliced at his throat. He died bloody and in pain. Her first true kill. Kai took the blade from her and told her to take a shower. She left him and the guys to handle the body.

7.57 AM

Madonna, Rhia thinks, *when I find you, your fate will be the same as Jang. And I command your fate.*

Fire in My Veins

Song Dedication: S.E.X by Lyfe Jennings

Blackstone Manor Shed
7.51 AM

Kai watched Rhia as she aimed the blade at Josiah's manhood. *Gotta say, if you want a man to talk, this would be perfect way.* "They call her *Madonna*. That's all I know. I swear." Poor man was shaking. Even he believed that she would let him go after she got the information. Instead, he saw a glint in her eyes and he knew Jang wasn't going anywhere.

"I know your brother was the pedophile, but you played with the girls before you sold them. Right?" Josiah closed his eyes and it almost looked like he was praying to the heavens. That was his mistake, because that told his wife that he did rape those girls. *Shit, to think what he could have done that to her.* Kai's fist clenched in anger and he wanted to kill him for Rhia. Before his eyes, Rhia took the blade and dug into his muscles. She split his dick into two flaps. Damn. Beside him, Sean and Paul covered their assets. Almost as if the slice had been made on them. Alek didn't even flinch as he stood near the door. Rhia chose well in her bodyguard and he hated to say that, but it was the truth. Then she cut through his neck and blood splattered across her. She didn't even notice the splatter as she handed him back his blade. He told her to go wash up. Seems corpse duty would be left to the three of them. Alek moved out of the way and opened the door. Rhia didn't even thank him which she had a habit of doing. Looking down at Josiah, Kai guessed he believed him now.

Blackstone Manor Shed
7.29 AM

When Kai entered the shed, Sean had been moments away from roughing up Josiah Jang. "Stop!" Sean had his fist raised and he knew if he hadn't come in time, he would have found a bloody Jang in his shed. That was not what he wanted. That wasn't what his wife needed. This was her demon and she would do as she wished with Jang. "You don't touch him. Rhia wants to speak with him." Jang laughed as if Rhia wasn't someone to be feared.

"Leaving your dirty work to a small woman. I didn't know you were such a coward, Blackstone." He smiled as if he won some game. *In my book Josiah was not the brains of the operation. Even after last night he thought Rhia was some harmless woman. Is he forgetting the threat she had handed him?* Or was he idiotic enough to believe she wouldn't go through with it? "So where is the little princess? She going to break a nail trying to spin me around for information?" Door number two, the man was simply stupid.

"Rhia is going to kill you and it won't be as easy as your brothers. In fact, I bet that you die screaming in pain." He didn't like Kai reminding him that his brother had died at Rhia's hands, yet he still laughed at Kai's words.

"Yeah, let's see if the whore has the guts for this," Jang simply challenged.

7.58 AM

He was burning in purgatory believing Kai now. *Sorry Jang,* Kai thought, *but you brought this on yourself. You helped unleash the deadly being hiding within Rhia.* As for himself, he had no complaints. He didn't have to worry about her pulling back at the last second. She may not like killing, but she would kill to protect those that she cared about now. They ended up burning Jang's body. It was a fitting death. Just as Rhia swore, he died being skinned alive and then roasted.

8.20 AM
Blackstone Manor

He walked inside to find his wife in the kitchen. She was cooking up a storm. Bacon, eggs, sausage, pancakes, orange juice, cranberry juice, and mixed berry juice sitting on the counter. Platters filled with food so that everyone could walk and get their own meal. Yet it was just them. Who was she cooking for? "Rhia, no offense darling, but we won't be able to eat all of this." She turned to face him. Her hair was flowing along with the wind. Her hunter green eyes bright with… happiness. She had exchanged her red V-necked shirt for a dark green V-necked shirt. She had on another black pair of skinny legs and black boots that hugged her legs. She was beautiful.

"Genny and Lucia will be here in a minute." He didn't hear the phone ring earlier.

"They called to say they were on their way?" She shook her head as she dug around, pulling out plates and bowls. "Did you call them?" She shook her head again, not minding him at all. So focused in preparing for a full house. He was about to ask her how she knew that they were on their way when she stood still for a split second.

"Who the hell is Emerson?" She didn't sound mad or scared, but the name rung off so many alarms inside his head. How did she know Emerson? Before he could throw her into a very complicated conversation, May Lin alerted them that they had a delivery. Standing outside was a kid with an envelope in his hands. The blue rose sigma told Kai exactly what was inside, and now he had to wonder if there was more to his wife's eyes than colors warning, because her eyes never flashed yet she *saw* this.

Dear Mr. and Mrs. Blackstone
You are invited to the Emerson Ball
Marakitza Hotel
8.00 PM Tonight.

Only those with the highest rank knew who Emerson was. He didn't rule a territory, but he would set up a meet when things were about to go disastrously wrong for all the United Territories. There hadn't been a meet in more than sixty years. Mother of the Sky! And the meet was there in Louisiana which meant their little warfare had just been put on everyone list of responsibilities. There wasn't even a crime lord that would ignore Emerson's call. Five minutes after the invitation, his mother and sister did show up and Rhia never said how she knew they were coming. Then, they didn't fully understand the power of her gifts. How could they? They were only beginning to show at that time.

5.10 PM

Kai said that they had some big ball to go to that night. So Rhia had called Priscilla up and said that she needed a major once over. Something that screamed Mafia Boss Wife, the *Dona*. Priscilla was on her way to give Rhia the full course. It really didn't help that she was running late. Rhia's nerves were swaying left and right. All day she had these flashes. They were like memories except she hadn't lived them yet. And she was praying that it was some flashes from her dreams and not like last time. Priscilla came through the door. She was carrying a dress bag and her make up kit. Her short red curls swished around her head. Her tall buxom body was dropping under all the weight in her hands. Her brown eyes clearly showed how tired and weak she was. She looked hazardous. "I know I'm late. Give me a second to set up and we can get started."

As Kai passed by them, he shouted, "Her hair needs to be up as much as possible." Priscilla rolled her eyes and pulled Rhia up the staircase. True to her gift, she gave a complete do over. Rhia began to relax and then Priscilla pulled out the dress. Rhia realized then she was in a waking nightmare. An off-the-shoulder, deep-purple formal dress that reached the floor. A low deep cut in the back. In the center designed by diamonds and rubies forms the magnolia flower in bloom. The flashes hit her hard. Heat. Glazed eyes. Room spinning. Pain. Sunlight. Bliss. The snap of chains. Her hands gripped the chair to keep her from falling. Rhia didn't want to wear that dress. If she did, she wouldn't wake up in the morning as one being. She didn't know what that meant or how she knew, but her gut and something old with a taste of primal was screaming inside her head. Priscilla watched her worriedly as she stared at the dress in Priscilla's hands. It was beautiful, but threads of fate cloaked around it. Shakenly, Rhia put on the dress. It fit her perfectly. Fearing what may happen that night, she didn't worry about the skin that she was showing off.

8.30 PM

Kai had on a full black Kandori suit. Standing in a room with only seven leaders, Rhia understood that this Emerson only called on the heads of Louisiana territory. Judging by the wary looks that Kai was given by some of the men, he understood that Emerson was going off-course for this meeting. And he didn't like the change. She wrapped her hand around his arm. He faced her and they... seemed to have this silent conversation. *I know. Even if I don't like it I'm not going make a move here.* His words seemed to move around inside her head and she thought she understood exactly what he wanted to say.

Good. She was glad for once that she could connect to someone so well that she could realize what they wanted to say without speaking. It didn't matter. She was focused on preventing her flashes from coming true. A waiter passed by and she snagged a cherry champagne. She needed something to soothe her nerves. Ignoring her senses, that found the feeling of the waiter familiar. Five minutes after she finished her drink, she didn't feel so well. Her body was burning. A fire was consuming her. Her heart was pounding within her chest. It hurt. Felt like it was punching outside her chest. She couldn't breathe. Where was the air? She could hear the rasp as she tried to catch her breath. She searched for Kai. He went to get her a snack before Emerson would make an appearance. Gods, she was burning up. She could feel the sweat drip from her body. And a throb deep within her lower regions.

"Alek…ge-get…Kai. Can't… I can't… breathe… so… damn… hot." Beside her, Alek was conflicted. She could tell he wanted to stay beside her, but he knew she needed Kai. Finally deciding to obey, he went to get Kai. Leaning against the bar stool, her skin itched. Her dress was too tight. She needed to take it off. *High Lord, Kai where the hell are you*? Like a magician, she could feel Kai wrapping his arms around her as he took her out of the ballroom. She couldn't focus. Everything blurred before her. Even Kai, but the silver and red aura told her it was him. She could see his aura. That was fascinating and scary, as she knew that it was him. It was the first time she saw his aura.

"Get us a damn room. Now," he demanded from someone. She didn't know who. She didn't care. *Someone cool her down, please.* As they moved to the elevator, Kai lifted her tighter into his arms. Good, because her legs were starting to feel like jelly. "Find me the person that gave her zodiac." Zodiac, the drugs they used to induce an unstable lust. The shit was worse than Essence and Blush combined. Gods help her. She wasn't prepared for this. Kai headed straight for the shower inside the room. Cold water hit her flamed skin. It didn't help. She burned more. There was a fire burning in her veins. As she looks at Kai, it burned like a forest fire. Unable to end. The water had soaked through his shirt and she could see beneath it. She knew what she needed. What she wanted. Grasping his tie and pulling him close, she kissed her husband. This burn. This need… she pushed it all into him. *Let's go up with the flames.*

Roses and Enemies

Song Dedication: Trouble I'm In by Twinbed

When Alek first walked into this room and he took in the faces of everyone, he could feel the temptation and trouble. His boss wasn't in any danger here, but something didn't feel just right. Everything seemed normal and was going fine. *Don* Kai even went to snag a snack for the *Dona*. However, a few seconds later, her skin flushed the deepest red he had ever seen. She clutched her chest in pain. She was breathing loudly and deeply. "Alek...ge-get Kai. I can't... can't breathe. So hot." Even her voice that was soft was lower than a whisper. He had never seen anything like this. Did he obey her order or stay? She swayed and gasped trying to catch her breath. Across the room, he saw the *Don* with his guards. Alek raced over to them.

"*Don*, *Dona's* not feeling well." Kai was moving before he could finish his sentence. He took a quick look at the *Dona* and grasped her by the arm. Pulling her away and out of the ballroom. His eyes flared with hate and Alek was glad to not be on the receiving end. He demanded a room and the person checking in people took one glance at his face and didn't argue. *Dona* was swaying even more on her feet as if she was drunk, but she only had a glass of champagne. She couldn't be drunk. *Don* lifted her into his arms as the elevator doors opened and they stepped in.

"Find the person that gave her zodiac." He commanded the three of them before going into the room. *Oh, shit!*

Kai thought that the cool water would help fight off the drug. Zodiac wasn't anything to play with. It made the victims feel a need for sex so strongly that they couldn't say no. It was a fucking date rape drug. And some bastard had slipped it to his wife. That was one bold man. One that he would personally kill. The water soaked them both. He was shaking with fury as he watched the water slide down her body. Her hunter-green eyes glanced up at him and it was pure hunter green. The white shade behind was coated hunter green. In that split second, his wife became the darkest predator he had ever faced and it was so sexy. Almost in slow motion, her fingers wrap around his tie and pull him in. The kiss was a solar eclipse. Brilliant light, sun, and fire pouring inside his body and soul as she pulled the cold and darkness from him into herself. He wrapped his arms around her waist and tangle their tongues together. His body became inflamed, his balls tightened, and his cock became hard. Shit! He pulled back. "Not like this. This isn't what you want, Rhia." And damn, but he didn't mean a word that he was saying. Her lips and tongue slid down his neck. She pulled his shirt from within his pants. Tugging on his belt, he trapped her hands against the shower wall. If he let her go any further, then there would be no stopping them both. Her lip graced his ear and she begged.

"Please... please... I... need." The soft low velvet voice taunted him. *Let's go up in flames.* By the heavens. A man could only take so much. He turned the shower off and dragged her into the bedroom. Lips and teeth clashed together. As Rhia finished unbuttoning his shirt, her lips kissed a pathway down. Heat scorched his skin. She unbuckled his belt, unzipped his pants and they dropped to the floor. Pulling her up, he softly kissed her. That fire burning inside of her was consuming them both. He unbuttoned her over the shoulder strap wrap and he found her zipper on the side. Slowly it crept down. Within seconds they were both naked. She was glorious. He wrapped his hands around her leg and pulled her into him. Her heat was close. Using his hands, he entered her core and its liquid heat. She was already ready for him. As he entered her slowly, inch by inch, she had a death grip on his shoulder.

Her fingernails dug into his shoulder blades. He kissed her like this was their last day on earth. He pulled the air from her lungs, her body, and her soul. He tangled their tongues together and swallowed her tears. Her pain. He caressed her. He touched. Each movement told her she was loved. That was okay to give. Her breath hitched and a moan escaped. He made slow, sweet love to her. He took away the pain and gave her the passion. Her skin flushed that deep red that he knew he would love to see from this day forth. She wrapped her legs tighter around him, forcing him into her more. Fire exploded inside the tiny room. As she had demanded, they went up in flames. For several hours, he touched her body, he kissed upon her, he gave all of himself to her. And they burned. He didn't recall how much time had passed. He didn't know when they finally found satisfaction and fell asleep.

The next morning, he woke to Rhia leaning against his chest. One leg thrown against his own and a smile curved her lips in her sleep. She breathed in softly, but deep. He moved her wavy black hair to the side and slowly her eyes opened to face him. Those clear, hunter-green eyes. Back to their normal peace. The wind breezed through and the scent of roses floated from her. She sat up, wrapping the sheets around herself. His lips quirked into a smile. He wanted to laugh. He knew the drug was the reason for what happened, but he wouldn't take it back for the world. Then she surprised him by turning around and giving him a peck on the lips before running off to take a shower. He did laugh out loud then. A knock sounded at the door. His peaceful moments were over, apparently. He found his boxers and pulled them on, as damp as they were. Opening the door, standing there, was Dwayne Emerson, the current speaker for the Emerson family. Emerson was in his late eighties. Black and white stripes of hair curled his head. Sky blue eyes. Heavy laughter lines. Even heavier weight.

"Since you were too preoccupied to make the meet, I came in person to give the news. *Madonna* works for the Royals. A new organization that believes in one ruling government. Sorry about what happen to your wife, and be careful." He walked away before Kai could ask him anything. Damn man. At least he was useful. Suddenly Kai's heart clenched and he knew that something was wrong with Rhia. Running inside the bathroom, he found her staring at her breast where a mark had appeared. A hunter-green rose with a red dagger cutting through the thorns. That wasn't there last night. As he moved to her and grab her by the arms, she looked down his arm and gasped. He looked down, wondering what the hell was going on, and he saw the same marking on himself. Except his rose was red, and the dagger is hunter green. *What has happened to us?* Her green eyes clashed with his in shock.

"I... I... I... c-ca-can... hear... you... inside my head." Her voice was shaky and she stuttered as she talked to him. He wasn't alone – this was the proof. Something had changed in them during that night. Some kind of bond had formed. One where death had no control over. *Rhia,* he felt the clash as her brain refused to acknowledge what she was seeing, and she fainted. He caught her and they crashed together. Holding her close, he wouldn't let her fall. Their future just became more complicated than fighting in a war.

Darling huntress, you're not alone. We are in this together. He didn't know why he called her huntress. It just seemed to fit her then. With Rhia in his arms, he waited for her return.

As Althea waved her hand on Dania's pond that allowed her to view her descendants' lives, she saw the mark. When a hunter found the soul that belonged to them. One who could heal them, accept everything that they are, and hold them together their own soul will recognize them and mark the two personally. However, the Huntsman Clan ancestors must first recognize the descendant and partner. As a daughter, Rhia should only be protected, never marked. They had claimed them both and made her a huntress. A vigilant being that defeated the dark and kept the balance of Earth. "Vikhtor, our Rhia is more than a queen. I don't know what these two will be able to do together, but I'm watching. And your clan protects them both." Darkness they may have walked, but light would prevail in them. Althea would watch her come into her name. Whatever name she may hold.

Bound

Song Dedication: Numb by Linkin Park

Rhia's eyes fluttered open and she came face to face with Kai. His arms surrounded her in warmth and held her close in protectiveness. Everything from last night until now flashed in her mind. She'd seen this before it even happened. "Is there more to your gift then what you told me?" Kai stared at her with sad eyes. The sadness was for her; she could feel that he was aware and that she was afraid and confused, and yet he could do nothing to ease her fears. That was what saddened him. And she wanted to crawl into a ball because everything that was happening was so different than what her aunt told her. Visions, the ability to see the future. Tattoos appearing upon her skin. Sharing a telepathic link with someone else. Not to mention being able to feel their emotions and know why they are feeling that way. All of these things her aunt never mentioned. "What about your father's family? Were they gifted?" She wondered how much could they *hear* now. Would there ever be another secret between them? What would become of this bond?

"My aunt never talked about my father or his family. I understood there was hate between them." And her mother crossed the line by loving her father.

"So, in order to understand your gifts more, we may have to track him down. Until then you need to tell me everything. Then again I may come to *know* at the same time as you." Yes, with this bond they had no idea what would happen to them. Kai may even have been able to see her visions with her. He pulled them up and as she faced the mirror, she saw the marks. They were new tattoos and she realized they were bound. That was what she was afraid of as she stared at that dress last night. It was the knowledge that she wouldn't ever be alone again. For some reason, they were tied, unable to break, even if they were to get a divorce. And that scared her more than waking the monster of her soul. His hand slipped under her chin and he faced her toward him.

"I'm catholic, darling. We don't believe in divorce." And he kissed her forehead and left her to shower.

It was nearly eight in the morning before they made it home. For some reason, Genny was standing in the floor room before the staircase when they walked in. She didn't say anything or ask them why they were late coming in. She walked up to Kai, stood up on her tiptoes and whacked him on the back of his head. "You are not missing Sunday Mass today. The both of you get dressed." *Excuse me?* Rhia wasn't Catholic. In fact, she didn't have any religion, so why was she going to Mass? Before she could ask Genny that, Kai grabbed her by her arm and dragged her up the steps to their room. He pulled his jacket off as he closed the door behind them. The click of the door closing makes her catch her breath. Although she had accepted Kai and everyone else, this wasn't her territory. Anything could happen and she liked escape routes. Kai just cut off the only route in this room. Maybe he was listening into her thoughts because a second later he cracked the door ajar. He watched her until she nodded her head in okay.

"Ma knows that you don't worship anything. Therefore, she intends to pull you into Catholicism. Please don't argue and come along." Since he asked nicely, she entered the walk-in closet and searched among her clothes. She came across a silk, long-sleeve cotton button-down white dress, along with white strap tan wedges. Seemed perfect for a church service. As she dressed, the flashes came in again. Smoke. Screams. Cries. Wails. Blood. Death. Collapse. Wood broken. Dismantled. She grasped the sink to keep standing. *Oh Heavens, someone help me.* Without her calling him, Kai came into the bathroom and just stood beside her.

"I don't know where or when but something awful will happen today." And as she looked up at him, she could see herself through his eyes. Her eyes were pure hunter green. She couldn't even see the white that normally hid behind a person's eye color. It left her shaking. She almost slipped, but Kai was holding her up. Keeping her together. Together they left the room. Alek and Sean were waiting for them outside the door. Both of them stopped mid step when they saw Rhia. When they saw her eyes. "You see it?" she asked. Sean didn't want to answer her question, but he admitted that he could see the strange color. Alek simply nodded and then stood beside her. When she chose Alek as her guard, she believed he was her ticket out of Blackstone. Now she wondered if a small part of her knew that she could never leave, so she picked someone who would always accept her and her decisions no matter what. No one else saw the strange color of her eyes. Just the four of them, and she wondered what that means.

They arrived at the church that held her wedding. The church that should have made her feel at peace even on a small scale now had her shivering and a desperate instinct telling her to run. She didn't. Rhia moved forward. She walked with her family and sat down to attend the service. She may not have been Catholic, but she would respect the religion. *If there is a High Lord in the sky, I ask for the first time in my life, whatever that will happen today spare the ones I care for.* She was not sure if anyone was upstairs listening, but for the first time in twenty-two years she took a leap of faith and prayed. She prayed all throughout the lecture. As they stood for the Profession of Faith, out of the corner of her eye in the church door she saw long, flowing blond hair tinged with red edges leaving the church. Red edges were the Blackstone trademark. She didn't want to disrupt the service, but someone leaving wasn't normal. She pulled on the elbow of Kai's sleeve. When he glanced at her, Rhia barely opened her mouth before the sweetest voice screamed, "Crow reaps gas!" and a second later the church shook as the bomb hits the windows and crashes inside. Crow Reaps Gas peeled away the skin and drained the tissue like acid, but you have to breathe or touch it for it to be activated. Panic consumed the church, but it was too late. They ducked down and covered their mouths to avoid being hit. Feet shook the floor as they tried to escape through the door. Children's muffled cries could be heard. Mothers gave their lives to protect their children. Some weren't so lucky, and Rhia heard their wail as they must have watched their children be consumed by shadow flames. Red stained the floor. She heard the creak of wood.

Kai, the church is going to collapse. We have to get out of here. A telepathic link was helpful in this situation. Grasping her hand, he pulled her up and she held onto Lucy. Each of them were holding someone, from their family to their guards who had escaped the gas. They tumbled out of the church, avoiding the burning bodies as much as possible. This was wrong. Someone attacked a church. Someone had allowed children to die. For what? Outside they watched as the clergy and priest escaped last.

And the church tumbled to the earth. Breaking and splintering. As Rhia glanced around, she saw the pain of the living. She took in their grief. This attack had cost. Why? Why would someone bomb a church? What did they get out of it? She saw the blond hair tinged with red edges. Rhia knew that person was involved somehow. She chased after her. Kai shouted her name and storms after Rhia. Sean, Paul, and Alek right behind him. This woman had killed innocents. Rhia's blood burned and her heart echoed as its beat slowed to a steady pace. Her feet carried her faster and Rhia tackled the woman at the corner of an alley. As Rhia flipped the terrorist to face her, she could see tan skin, golden hazel eyes that shone with hate. "Why did you do it?" The terrorist laughed in Rhia's face.

"The *Madonna* does as she pleases. It is her right as the princess of Royals." *Madonna*. Princess. *Royals*. The woman was in that organization. They had gone too far this time. Rhia pulled her arm back. She was going to snap *Madonna*'s neck.

"Maya..." Kai's shocked whisper stopped Rhia. Maya... Maya Blackstone. I *was about to kill my cousin-in-law*. As she stared into Maya's eyes, Rhia realizes Maya was only a child herself. This was outside her boundary. Rhia stood up and allowed Kai to step forth. As the *Don* of the Blackstone Family, it was his decision to make on what to do with Maya. For once, Rhia was glad to not be in his shoes. He might have had to kill her.

The Don's Crown

Song Dedication: Can you Hold Me by NF

Sunday, May 29

The ride back home was filled with tension. Sean kept a steady eye on those of them sitting in the back. Paul had put the autodrive on military resistance, therefore he had to drive. Alek sat between his wife and Maya, his fourteen-year-old cousin who apparently was *Madonna* and had just blown up a church. Although Kai's uncle had always tested Kai's patience for authority, this was beyond his thread to bare. And worst, he believed that Maya was acting on her own authority. In the end, as Head of the Blackstone, it was his responsibility to decide her punishment. Yet she hadn't attacked the family, which could be covered up. She had attacked the people of Bossier City that were under Kai's protection. So, her punishment had already been decided even if he hadn't spoken it. Maya would die very soon. And by his hands. He wanted to close out the world. Someone's hands grasped his own tightly. He didn't have to look to know who they belonged to. Rhia. She was the only thing keeping him sane at the moment.

Back there in the alley, she had understood that she needed to take a step back. And she didn't try to pester him with questions on the way back. *Madre*... when she had seen Maya being dragged down the streets, held tightly by Alek and Sean, she had almost fainted. Because she had known. One look and his *Madre* had known what Maya had done. He wouldn't be surprised if she was calling his uncle at this moment in her own car. Once they reached the house, he pushed Rhia toward the front door. His *Madre* for once was inside before anyone else. Rhia glanced back at him. Her hunter-green eyes were normal again. Her white dress moved with the wind. She looked like an innocent child. He didn't know exactly what she was searching for in his eyes, but after a few minutes of staring, she finally went inside. Alek followed right behind her. In the last few days, Kai had come to realize why his wife chose him. She had instincts that even she wasn't aware of, but she listened to them. Alek… when he found the one he was loyal to, it was forever. Should something happen to him, Kai didn't have to worry about Rhia, because Alek would protect her until his dying breath. "Head to the shed. We know that she has information. Let's see if we can get it out of her." And his voice was cold. Maya had made her decision. She created and acted on her own move. Therefore, as of this moment she was not family. Not one of his blood. She was the enemy and… a lump filled his throat… he would end her. He walked behind Paul and Sean as they dragged her kicking and screaming.

Before Rhia entered their home, she stared at Kai. *Would he be okay with his actions?* she wondered. She looked and stared and slowly his sickly yellow aura appeared. She knew that wasn't his normal color. He was not okay with what he would have to do. Therefore, her next action was how to keep him sane. How could she help him stand? Only Genny may have known that answer. So, Rhia went inside to find her. And stopped in shock. Genny was in the kitchen pulling out food and pans. She was a bustle of nerves, this petite older woman who may have faced more than Rhia had lived. And Rhia wanted to comfort her. "*Madre…*" she called out. Genny told Rhia to call her that from day one, but Rhia couldn't. It didn't feel right until this moment. Genny was washing vegetables when Rhia called out to her. Genny stopped and Rhia saw her shoulders shaking. Rhia walked over to her, and Genny turned and hugged Rhia tightly. Silent tears flowed down her face. Rhia soothed her as best as she could.

"This will kill a piece of him. There are many things in this world that we can live with but taking out your own blood that is something no decent human being can live with even out of necessity." Yes, Rhia didn't have a living blood relative that she knew of. However, the thought of killing one because they had crossed the line. Rhia wouldn't be able to do that. And Kai didn't have a choice. He was the *Don*. Head of the Blackstone Family. And the crown that lays upon his head demands that he make the decision and act on it. She forced Genny to take a seat in a chair.

"What can I do to help him? He needs to keep going, but Maya may have ended everything." And Genny looked up at Rhia. Rhia could see it in her eyes. There really wasn't anything that she could do. Kai would have to fight this demon and rise above it on his own. "You can only be there for him." Genny rubbed her small hands against Rhia's cheeks and through her thick curls. "You must stand by him. And wait until his fight is over. Then you lift him back up." Her hands shook and she stood. "I'll cook tonight. You go prepare for his return." And Rhia obeyed because this was her family, and if Kai fell, they all might go down. Rhia would make sure he got back up. As Genny said, she could only lift him up after he was done fighting.

Paul strapped Maya into a chair while Kai pulled out his kit. It had all the tools he may need for an interrogation. This was the first time he would be using it against his family. Kai saw the Swiss spikes and passed over them. Xavier daggers were too big for what he needed to do. What could he use to make this swift and get answers quickly? He came across his needles and poisons. Angels' poison was the slowest activating poison. It took an hour to manipulate its will and activate the deadly toxins. It was incredibly painful. And an hour was long enough to receive the antidote. As Kai filled the needle with poison, he talked to Maya. "I'm sure you know what Angels' poison does to the human body. I'm going to slip you a little and, in an hour, if you haven't said anything, I'll give you the antidote and a larger amount of the poison than before. It's your decision to drag out your painful death." He pulled at her long sleeve shirt tails until it was at her elbow. And then he injected her with the poison and stepped back. Maybe he was going easy on her. Not roughing her up. Not asking questions. Not giving her the full dose. It may not seem like it, but that was the only kindness that he could show her. However, Maya was a Blackstone. They were stubborn and were fighters. Hours passed with the repeated process. She would scream and cry, but she wouldn't spill. Night was coming and blood drizzled from her eyes, nose, and ears. If she started coughing up blood, it was game over.

"Maya, I get it. Someone promised you power. They lied. Don't let your death be for nothing." He was trying his damnest not to mark her. Yet she was being so difficult.

"*Pensi di aver vinto. Essa deve vendicare la mia morte.*" And that was how his fourteen-year-old cousin gave her last breath. He couldn't help it. He screamed and it echoed in the shed. Filled with hate, frustration, and hopelessness. *You think you've won. She shall avenge my death.* Those were Maya's last words. So, who was *she* that Maya spoke of? Kai could hear the air move in and out of his body. Paul and Sean stood on the sidelines waiting for his next command. "Clean her up. I'm sure my *Tio* Dev will want her body back." And with an aching heart he returned to his room.

8.43 PM

Rhia felt Kai's pain and she knew that Maya had passed. She had already run a hot bath for him. While nothing could soothe the ache in his soul and heart, the warm water would do his muscles some good. He hadn't rested that day, and after running all day he would need it. Kai staggered into their room. His aura was tinged black with his normal silver and red. He pulled at his gray and white tie, only he couldn't seem to get it off. He pulled, tugged, and twisted but it wouldn't come off. He choked. Rhia ran to him and stopped his hands. He gazed at her and there was nothing in his eyes. Everything was blank. She didn't think he even saw her until she touched him. Slowly, like helping a lost child, she loosened his tie and pulled it over his head. She tugged on his hand until he followed her into the bathroom. She helped him undress and settled him into the bath. Then, gently, Rhia took a towel and scrubbed at his arms, shoulders, and back. For a few minutes, there was silent peace. Then his voice was so quiet she could barely hear him.

"She died holding the Royals' secrets. We got nothing out of her." And that was what was tearing him apart. That Maya not only died by his hands, but that she died loyal to someone that wasn't family. The Blackstone had their issues, but they stood together as family against their enemies. Today their enemy was one of their very own. She did the only thing she thought would help. She dropped the towel in the water. She slid into bath in her white veil nightgown and she held him. She held him as she had never held anyone. As she once wished someone would hold her. He broke in her arms. The pain and guilt that he was holding inside he let go. She couldn't hear or see his tears. She felt his body as he let the waterworks flow. And that was what he needed. A man could cry, but he couldn't always show it to others. Not when so many depend on him keeping a level head. She leaned her head against his back and she waited. She waited for her husband to end his inner battle. When she could no longer feel him shaking, she pulled them both up. She dried his hair and his body without a word. Now was not the time for words. When she faced him, she forced his eyes to look into her own. And she told him, "They will pay. We will make them pay for using a child. No one manipulates the young. No one *plays* with our *family*." With her words, her husband, the *Don*, came back. The pieces of his soul knitted back together. Three time tighter. Five times stronger. The Royals had made a huge mistake in becoming their enemy. They were alphas. They were the Silver Wolves Mafia. THEY WERE HUNTERS. And the Royals were prey to be hunted.

"She is creating a living Huntsman Clan. Any whose fate lies with her bloodline shall see the truth behind the shadows. The problem is..." Daerhae started to say but Althea already knew. With creation comes challenge. Tests that will try to twist Rhia's will. The biggest test was the Royals and even Althea did not know who they were. It is wrong that the child had to end as she did. However, for Kai and Rhia to unite and stand as one there will come many sacrifices. Althea only hoped that the two of them are ready. That they will be able to get pass this.

Shadows of Truth

Song Dedication: Stand by You by Marlisa

Blackstone Manor
June 1, 3034

The doors to the manor were opening, yet the silence inside was deafening. Kai was holding Maya's wake inside of their home. Everyone who attended knew that Kai had ended her life, yet not all knew that Maya was behind the Bossier Church Massacre, as they were calling it. Mostly the inner family and some organization members were aware of the circumstances. The Elders had stated that they were here to attend, but Maya wouldn't receive the respectful standing they normally gave the dead. The result was that Kai had sent *Madre* and Lucy into the kitchen with Rhia. Cooking for the dead wasn't easy. Cooking for the living – that was even worse. Cooking for the living that come to grieve for the dead and scorned the events of their death had Rhia checking the door every fifteen seconds to see that Kai was okay. He was greeting guests in his black Kandori suit. It wasn't as crisp and perfect as she had come to see. There were wrinkles as stark as the ones in his face.

    She was taking out the cornbread from the oven when they stepped through. One she recognized instantly; Devon Blackstone. The other man was short in stature. Possibly five feet exactly. Golden blond hair, white caucasian, hazel-green eyes and a hundred and ten pounds. Kai stood taller and an ice-cold look entered his eyes. He wasn't doing that for Devon. "*Madre* I'll be back in a second." Placing the pan on the countertop and leaving the towel to the side, Rhia's black heels echoed as she moved to stand beside Kai. She didn't know this man, but she knew he wasn't welcomed. She pulled at the tips of her long-sleeved dark gray shoulder span dress.

"Elias Santiago, I wasn't expecting to see you here." And Kai meant it. Friends, family, and associates were allowed inside for the wake. Yet Elias Santiago wasn't on any of those lists. Rhia remembered Kai talking about this man. At the time, he was warring with Josiah over Blanchard and Alexandria. With Jang out of the way, the territories should have been easy to pick up only Alexander had taken Alexandria for some reason. Kai was meeting him later tonight to get an understanding of the situation. Santiago must have been aware that the big three heads of Louisiana had united as one in a way. A fight with Alexander was a fight with them. It would be more than foolish to try especially on a day like this.

"My pal Vincent Coulter told me of the grievous mishap. I've come to pay my respects. It's wrong for someone so young to die." Devon jerked next to him as if he had been hit.

"Yeah, and we all know who to blame for that darling nephew." Devon spat at Kai's suede shoes. "Thanks to the Blackstone name, my baby girl is going to the ground in a few days." His eyes flashed with rage and he pulled out an Azai 22. Tears filled his eyes and Rhia could see them so clearly. "I've buried many people in my life, but I'll be damn if I lay my daughter to rest and not send her *murderer* with her." His voice was loud and stretched throughout the house. Santiago stood to one side and watched it. Almost as if he had planned for this.

Rhia crept to the edges and moved sideways so that she was behind Devon. She understood his grief, but you didn't point a gun at the head of your family. She pulled out the Xavier dagger she had carried with her. She moved to hit him at his lower back and Kai looked at her.

Don't. Kai's voice echoed inside her head. Like a shimmering whisper that was filled with the strength of iced steel. Cold and unbreakable. *He's threatening everything you stand for. Your title. Your authority. If you allow this Santiago will take it as a sign of weakness and attack.* She knew why he didn't want to, but their positions were forcing their hands.

Knock him down. I'll handle the rest. And as the *Don,* his word was law. Rhia had come to accept and obey that. She may not like it and wish to do the opposite, but Kai had been in this game longer. Plus, this situation wasn't normal. So, she found Devon's pressure point in his neck and hit it. Devon crashed toward his knees. For the next five minutes, he couldn't get up without help. Kai snatched the gun from his hand and held it steady, staring down at it. "If I had my way, I would have sent Maya to you to be imprisoned until she reached the age of thirty. Maya didn't give me a choice. She endangered the lives of innocents. She was active in the war against the Royals. And she betrayed **us**." Kai looked up at his uncle. The cold fire that breathed in his lungs was there for all to see. "When you fight against the family, when you threaten the family, small or big, no matter who you are, it is I, the *Don,* who must deal out your punishment."

And while he was staring in the eyes of his uncle so that he could see the man that adorned the crown, Devon thought he should be *Don,* but he wasn't made for it. Devon crumbled as if understanding what Kai had to go through in order to protect their family and organization. "That's why I won't apologize. I will grieve with you. I'll pray that the Mother in the Sky will open her arms to Maya, but that is it. For this family I will do anything." He took the Azai 22 flips it over and smashed it against Devon forehead. Blood trailed down. "For the Blackstones I am cold-blooded. If you strike against us expect to be hit back." Kai wasn't really talking to Devon any more. He was sending a message to everyone in the manor. Including Santiago. And Santiago didn't look happy at the speech with his lip pressed together. Kai's eyes circled the room, staring down everyone. Paul made the first move. Bowing down to his knee. He was showing his acknowledgment of Kai's authority and his loyalty. Slowly, the men and women who were of the Blackstone organization and family went to their knees. Some people who were not a part of the organization bowed down their heads at Kai's strength. And a new title was gifted to her husband that day. He became the First of the Kings. The Kings of Louisiana.

It was a moment that made Louisiana history, yet only a few knew what happened to create those men. And there were some things that the people of Louisiana were not aware of. Like her husband turning around and handing an ultimatum to Devon. "Someone used Maya. They made her a weapon of war. And they will pay by our hands. Are you a Blackstone or not?" It may have seemed like a simple question, but it wasn't. If Devon denied Kai, then he would be thrown to the streets. Forced to fend for himself and no chance of revenge for Maya. If he accepted Kai, then he could never again go against his commands. Shakes quaked his body. It was a twisted, deadly reality that they lived in, but Devon had to make the first move.

"Yes. I want them to pay. I want their blood on my hands. I want to cast them to hell for the death of my daughter." With that chess piece crashed into the game, Rhia helped Devon up. She didn't like Devon, but he understood family. And for the first time in years, the Blackstones were truly united as one more than a family, more than an organization; this was a King's army forged together. Standing beside each other against the enemy.

Empress thought that if Kai killed Madonna then it would cause a rift in the Blackstone's Family that would help her end them sooner. Since that plan was a bust, maybe she should activate the next weapon. She needed to break the Blackstones first, but so much was going off course. Alexander and Francesco had joined hands with Blackstone. Maybe if all else failed she could use Rhia to kill Malachi Blackstone. A laugh bubbles up in her throat. Wouldn't it be fitting if the wife that he had forced to marry him and had no feelings for him was the one to stab him in the heart? With that thought in mind, Empress steps outside of Blackstone Manor.

Seer's Sight

Song Dedication: Unthinkable by Alicia Keys

Blackstone Manor
June 3, 3034
Maya's Funeral Day

"Are you going to wear that again?" Rhia asked, standing behind Kai. Looking down at the black tie, he realized that he had adorned this suit for the past three days. The wrinkles were even visible in the dark and that was just shameful on his part. Rhia was holding up a black Kandori suit with a gray and black striped tie. "I wasn't sure if it had simply escaped your thoughts or if you were punishing yourself." He dropped the black tie from his hands and began to unbutton his dress shirt. Rhia was dressed in a long-sleeve, black, button-down dress that reached her knees. A dark brown belt tied to her waist and brown flats. She was patient and quiet while holding one of his other suits. These last few days throughout the wake she had been doing just that. Mostly he was grateful. The other day so much had changed because of Maya's death and the only real constant was Rhia. Even *Madre* and Lucy's persona had shifted on a small level. He had noticed that they both now carried weapons with them whenever they stepped out the door. Although *Madre* didn't cry, the heart-breaking look in her eyes told everyone that she wasn't okay with this war or the deaths. She had lived with his father more than forty years and the death and blood that stained his hands, while she had been aware of it, she had never seen. And now Death was a cold winter front blowing into the south. Rhia was twisting the tie around his neck when she froze. Her eyes glazed over and the world hidden inside of her frosted over in cloudy ice shards. She shook, she swayed, and she collapsed into his arms.

"What did you see?" The bond had opened many doors inside of their minds, but her visions escaped him. That was hers alone to see and tell.

"I didn't exactly see, but I heard a voice. The past and present collide. Friends and family tied, but the enemy twist and the innocence is stained. The weapon wielded shall strike against your heart and blacken your soul." It was a warning, but none of it made any sense.

"We're going to the Dust Fields. More than anyone else you need a Neptune's Reading." He had set it up for her to have one when questions of her parentage and gifts had started rising. He didn't think she would consent to one considering the price.

"Can we afford such a reading?" Yeah, for most people the price was too much. A hundred and fifty thousand can cut anyone's pocket. That's why only the desperate and rich were willing to pay for it.

"I managed to get a discount, and Rhia we really need answers before your powers become worse." It may have been just visions for now, but there could be more.

It was a knife to his heart watching Maya be laid to rest. He didn't know if the High Lord and Mother of Sky was listening to their silent pain, but a storm was brewing. The oak tree branches were cracking under the wrath of the wind. The sky darkened to a deep gray. They twist and spin of circled clouds. Although there was no rain, the sound of thunder boomed and clapped and struck at the sky. It was like giving voice to the Family Blackstone's grief and rage. The crowd dispersed slowly and they walked back to the three Moxac autodrive waiting at the cemetery curb. "Paul, go back with my mother. We're heading to the Dust Fields for a reading." The Dust Fields only had the Neptune's Reading. And they didn't need as much protection in the Dust Fields. It was neutral territory and reigned by the darkest mutations from the Campris Wars.

3.48 PM
Dust Fields

They didn't call it Dust Fields for no reason. It was once the rumored downtown of Louisiana. However, when the radioactive bombs crashed, there were too many tall buildings in the way. They fell into shadows of dust. Very few buildings survived that day. Harlem's Portrait did and was now standing by use of Hollow Glow, neonites that they used to build our steel homes today. Inside the autodrive, Rhia could see the famous painting. A picture that showed joined nationality. An elderly woman whose gray tips were showing with white pearl earrings and with a blue gown on. She was looking down at a photo album. A haggard, white, middle-aged woman. Her arms cradled beneath her head, holding her together. A flowing water fountain with a small black child hiding behind it. The rest of it didn't make it. The Old Crave had manage to survive. Light gray stone made the outside with clear tall windows. Inside the beige, square, thick walls keep it standing. A ten-foot-long and four-foot-wide table stood in the front. You placed your hands on the surface and the Priestess bound and saw all. Rhia was afraid of what the Priestess would say, and she really wanted a private reading upstairs, but that would cost more, and Rhia was sure they had paid more than enough. Kai grasped and held tight to her left hand. She took a deep breath and layed her right hand upon the table.

Rhia Ambria Dashayani RiverBlood

Born: October 31, 3011

Mother: Ashlynn Mahajan of the Ashfer's Soldiers

Named heir of Matilda Ravina, 3rd princess to the English Alliances, mother of Ashlynn Mahajan

Father: Ethan Halden of the Hunter's Clan

Race: East Indian/Scottish

Titles: Dona to the Blackstone Family, 2nd princess to the English Alliances, Huntress of the Halden Clan.

Marks: O souls

Powers: Huntress, pyrotamer, and True Seer

As the power-filled voice had spoken, the table drew her blood in. It was the most painful thing that she had ever felt. Like sucking in her very essence and spitting her heart outside of her being. She gasped and tightened her grip on Kai's hand. Rhia thought the Priestess was done, but her voice became louder and echoed.

Destiny: To free Vikhtor the first hunter, First Queen of Louisiana, and one of the four keys to destroy the Sovereign leader of the Royals.

Rhia's knees quaked and buckled. *High Lord, oh goddess, oh Mother of the Sky*, she felt sick. Her insides repelled and she couldn't take it any more. She dashed outside and spilled her lunch to the ground. They shouldn't have come. Knowledge is power and now too many knew her own. A true seer. *Oh, damn.*

She was fucked. She was screwed. She wanted to scream to the heavens. Hadn't fate cast enough stones on her life? Rain pounded down from the sky. Thunder shakes the clouds. Striking, aiming, pushing… she heard Kai's voice in the background. He tumbled into her and pushed them but it was not enough. Lightning hit them and fused into their being. A fire scorched their veins and pulled them into the dark abyss. They crashed and darkness consumed them both.

Innocence Strikes

Song Dedication: Stole by Kelly Rowland

9.14 PM
Blackstone Manor

The first thing that Kai knew upon awakening was pain. Electrical shocks flowed through his bloodstream. People don't talk about what they feel when struck by lightning. There was a numbness going from his fingertips and to the soles of his feet. The back of his neck and shoulders burned like liquid fire had been thrown on it. Thank Mother he had asked Sean to activate a Black Ring device, or the information about Rhia would be in the wrong hands as of this moment. As he leaned up to a sitting stance, he noticed that Rhia and he were in their master bedroom at the manor. Someone had sprawled them against their bed. Red gold flames surged against the edges of Rhia's dress. The mystery of his wife was driven inside of an impenetrable wall. Only a few were welcomed inside. It didn't make their responsibilities easier. The war. Her powers. The changes of titles. For more than a hundred years the world has been stagnant and now everything was shifting and changing. He hadn't a clue what exactly was going on, but he knew that they would survive. Question was did they want to be here for the new world? Some would say living no matter how different that is what you wished for more than anything. What if living meant being there for the end? Would you want to live when everything else that was familiar was no longer there with you?

Rhia's eyes fluttered open and panic registered first. He could feel her instinct to run. To get as far away as possible. She leapt up and made a start for the door. He wrapped his arms around her arms and waist. She kicked up, screaming. Her feet dangled and she pinpointed and hit his shin. He almost dropped to his knees. Her head crashed backwards and hit the center of his forehead. Dazed with blinding light, his grip loosened and her right arm was freed. She elbowed him in his ear and he completely let go of her. She twisted and he saw for the first time that Rhia wasn't normal. Her eyes had changed the color of deep purple and there was panic clouding them. Her breath was short and rapid. She was in a fighting stance. Fists balled together, arms crossed and lowered, feet planted and turned slightly inward. Anyone else in this stance would easily be defeated, but Rhia was a true born fighter. Any odds that came her way would find out that the unexpected was her sole advantage. Because she refused to submit to rules, she was able to defy all and succeed. And that fighter was blinded in panic and locked in a room with him.

Before he could move, she flew. The Red Wing was known for her speed. So fast that the human eye couldn't see. They didn't lie. He couldn't see anything, but he did sense what she was going after. She jumped and twisted with her leg out. The back end of her foot connected with the tip of his head. A second and a much harder kick collapsed onto his shoulder. He felt that crack as it was dislocated. She spun around behind him and kicked at his feet to knock him down. He almost didn't notice the dagger coming toward his chest. He grasped her arm tightly in his hand. She couldn't see or hear me. How did he snap her out of the cloud of panic?

You are her anchor. The huntress listens, but you must call her. Call the hunt away.

He really didn't have time for this shit. War. Powers. And now voices inside of their heads. He didn't know who they were, but they seem to be helping both Rhia and him. How exactly was he supposed to call the hunt away? With Rhia using all her strength to push the small dagger into his chest? *Damn she's strong!* He didn't recall her being capable of such strength. He clenched his teeth and pushed with all his strength in his hope to flip her over to ground. They were both in a sitting stance when the dagger sliced against his skin and made him bleed. Rhia blinked and the purple of her eyes became lighter. She went under a little and then he tugged on the dagger to get it out of her hands. He was allowing so much pressure within his body that he didn't feel when his teeth grazed against his lip and cut it. The purple was very light that he could now see the green as a background color. The dagger flew and struck into the wall near the walkin closet. Rhia went down, crashed against the floor with him above her holding her wrists tightly in his hands. Rhia blinked and her hunter-green eyes flashed back. She stared up at him in confusion.

"Kai, what's going on?" Her voice was as soft as it was when they first meet. That velvet whisper slipping back into her words. And he knew his Rhia had returned. Something had possessed her in her panic. A huge deep breath escaped him.

"Mother of the Sky, do not ever and I mean never do that to me again." A shudder moved through my body. "In simple words, you panicked."

"Panicked!" Rhia didn't know the feeling of panic. Kai wasn't making any sense. Yet she didn't remember anything after lightning hit them. She glanced over at Kai. Even in the old world, being hit by lightning was almost always a death sentence. Yet the both of them were alive and breathing. "I panicked?" He could hear the question in her words.

"Yes, earlier you thought that everyone heard your Neptune's Reading. I should have told you that I activated a Black Ring and maybe we wouldn't be having this conversation. I apologize." His eyes were clear in their sincerity. More importantly, no one but the four of them knew the truth. For once she was very grateful. She didn't know if she should laugh or cry. In a very big way, she was a Warrior Princess. And you could bet she had no wish to be another Xena. She didn't know what life Xena lived in the old world, but she would not be repeating it. She glanced over at the clock. The pitch-black shades that they never used were covering the window. It was really late. "I need to wash up and cook dinner." As she stood, Kai grasped her smaller hand with his much larger one.

"Mom probably cooked today. Let's just clean up and make our own dinner. Give yourself a rest. We both deserve one." That was right. They did need a rest. A lot had happened that day. Finding out her past. Facing her future. And above all, they put Maya to rest. There were shadows and dark bags in Kai's eyes. Although he didn't look haggard, he must have felt raw from the day's events. She tightened his hold on her hand.

"Join me," she commanded as she helped him to his feet. While Kai made a bath for them, she searched among their clothes for sleepwear. She decided on a V-necked peach nightgown that reached her thighs. Gold etching of diamonds and sapphires. And black, silk boxers. Kai didn't have her taste for old world clothing, but they were slowly growing on him.

"Bath is ready," she heard him say from behind her.

Grabbing their clothes, she laid them neatly on the counter of the sink. With her back facing Kai, he unzipped her dress. In the mirror, out of the corner of her eye, she saw a black and gold scorpion on the floor near the bath. Its stinger flat to the ground and claws closed tightly. She would have been startled except that it was very clear to see that it was mechanical.

"Is that a Silver Star Shield Glass?" When activated, an invisible force field would stand in its place of defense.

"Yes," he said as he slowly pushed her sleeves forward to slide down her arms.

"Is that really necessary?" She meant seeing as they were inside their own home. Her dress sounded like a soft thump as it hit the floor. In the mirror, his chocolate brown eyes shone with a hunger as he unsnapped her bra.

"Better to be precautious. Not like we haven't been attacked at home before." His fingers flowed over her lace purple panties and he slowly dragged them down her legs. She could feel his breath against the back of her thighs and her own breath hitched inside her lungs. A slow burn crept up her body. He stood and turned her toward the bath. Without a word, she stepped inside. The heat soaked into her skin pores. Ninety degrees and light suds. The perfect bath. She leaned against the side of the wall and faced the back of Kai. He took off his silver cuff-links, pulled off his black jacket. Then he unsnapped the buttons at the wrist of his shirt and began to unbutton the rest. Kai had the perfect silent persona of a mafia boss. In a dark way, it was enchanting and addictive. Then again, darkness itself is consuming. Slowly swallowing you in until you don't wish to escape. That was the kind of darkness that made up Kai. She didn't think she could live without that darkness. As he tugged on his shirt to pull it off, there was a new mark upon him. She instinctively moved to touch it, but he was standing too far away. "What is it?" He must have seen her move in the mirror.

"Flames. Living flames licking up at the top of your back. It goes all the way across. It's red gold. On your left shoulder blade is a white clover colored and some words I don't understand." It was beautiful yet dangerous. That was what it looked like to her.

"As best as possible tell me what it says." She could see the words colored in hunter green. She got this weird feeling they were about her.

"*Quando la morte di lei tira in caccia, che io chiamo le spalle alla luce.*" As he unzipped his slacks, anger clouded his face.

"When Death pulls her into the hunt, I call her back to the light." It was about the both of them. Whatever the markings were, their meaning was for the both of them.

"Turn around." No need to ask why. The last one that appeared on them it was in a very similar fashion. She faced the wall. She heard the soft steps of his feet. Her mouth clamped down to lock her breath inside. She feared that there was another mark upon her. He slid into the bath and his arms wrapped around her waist. His lips touched the end of her neck and in the center of her back.

"You don't have one." She breathed heavily from relief and from the desire that had been awakened in them. His hands encircled her breast, and she could feel the powerful throb of him beneath her. She dipped back and he sucked on her shoulder. Her breath rasped and her hands pulled at his as he twisted her nipples. "Give in," he said, and her blood surged. His lips traced against her back. His teeth pinched slightly. Finally, his hands released her and spun her around, her knees on each of his sides and she sat before him. His fingers intertwined in her black locs and he pulled her in for a kiss. Tongues collided; he sucked on her lips. Fire raced through them and they burned. She scraped her sharp nails down his chest. He tugged at her hair strands until their eyes met. Sitting up and wrapping her legs around him, he thrust deeply inside her heat. She gritted her teeth at the first sharp pain and bit his neck until she drew blood. He didn't slow down any. The pace was fast. Water sloshed around them. The thickness. The hardness. Repeatedly pushed through. Tearing against her wall. She panted. She gasped. Her arms around his neck were the only thing keeping her up. His hands pulled on her waist. Pushing her core onto him.

Light struck through her and blinded her sight. She pushed and her right hand landed against the shield. A small tingle surged into her bloodstream. Their lips locked, tongues twisting, teeth clashing, and breath was exchanged for breath. Fire spilled and exploded around them. They rose to the sky and slowly descended back to the earth. Kai still had her wrapped around him as they came through. They were breathing deeply and loudly. A small smile graced her face. The building force from the day's events shook from their bodies with their release. He leaned back against the bathtub. Kai seemed a little more relaxed than he had been for the last few days. She allowed him to slip outside of her now that they had both been sated. She soaked up a towel and began to clean herself in front of him. Kai watched her with his head cocked upon his hand on the edge of the tub. At the lower end of her thigh, she found her new marking. They hadn't noticed it before. On her left ankle was a tiny white clover with a black and gold chain bound tightly around it and a ring of red gold fire surrounding it. *I caccia I vivi dannati nel buio e le sue ombre mi tira via dal fuoco del"inferno.*

Kai's eyes tracked the words, reading and translating in his head. "I hunt the damned living in the darkness and his shadows pulls me away from hell's fire." And then she understood what it was all coming down to. Halden Clan of Hunters. This was her father's legacy, whatever that may be. Kai pulled her into his chest, and she lay her head there, gathering her thoughts. That was how they stayed until the water cooled. They went to bed without dinner. Neither of them felt hunger after that realization.

June 4, 3034
7.13 AM

Rhia woke to sun shining through the shades. She was alone inside of the bed. There was a note on the bed. In Kai's fancy handwriting, it stated that he had a meeting with Alexander and Francesco this morning. He would be back before ten that morning. She stretched and sat up. Looking around her clothes, she found a yellow button-down dress to the waist that flowed out wide until it reached her knees. Color. For today she needed color. They had adorned enough black and gray. Just for a few hours, with the bright sun she would shine. As she adorned the dress, that hollow voice crept inside of her head and deep within her mind. *For today, be careful of the old and face the new.* As time went on and her powers pushed through, she started to wonder who spoke to her and she wanted to shout to the skies that she hated her. Warnings, she had dealt with those her entire life. Foreseeing the future and having no way to change it. She may never have gotten used to that. Downstairs inside the kitchen, she stirred the pancake mix. Two batters. One with chocolate chips and another with blue berries. Sausage was cooking in the oven. Scramble eggs on a slow burn on top the stove. The plates all ready to be set up for when the food was done.

The doorbell rang as she poured the eggs into a large bowl. A few seconds later, Alek entered the kitchen. "*Dona*, I apologize for disturbing you, but a Mari Alvarez is asking to see you." He looked stoic as he gave his response. Her mind lapsed. Mari. Little Mari. She raised Mari the first five years after Mari came to the orphanage at three. Brunette curls. Pink lips and pale cheeks. Wide, brown eyes filled with mischief. Rhia didn't think about how Mari found her after being separated for eight years. With light filling her heart, she quickly moved to the living room where they hosted guests. Mari looked the same as when Rhia had last seen her. Long brown curls. Deep pink lips and white pale skin coated in red freckles. An oddity if Rhia had ever known one. She didn't see the cold wary look in Mari's brown eyes. No, she saw it, but she ignored it. Mari was taller than Rhia. Mari must have been at least five-ten. Mari had on a long sleeve black V-neck sweater and plain black jeans with flat black boots. Again, Rhia ignored the fact that although it was not terribly hot outside, it was also not extremely cold considering what Mari had on. Rhia pulled Mari close into a hug and asked Alek to give them some privacy.

"What on earth are you doing here?" It had been years and Rhia wanted to hold the memory of this moment.

"I needed to speak to you. There is a charity organization that I was hoping you would help." Rhia gestured for Mari to sit down and nodded her head.

"Tell me about it," she said.

"They are very nice people who are trying to do their best for the country. This country is ruled by gang leaders, drug lords, mafia, and mobsters. The fact that they rule and fees are collected are the reason the weak are becoming defenseless. If we had a powerful voice to speak on behalf of the weak." As Mari spoke, wariness slipped beneath Rhia's skin. What Mari was saying sounded like…

"We need a voice to show the weak that if they band together, they will be stronger than those who use and kill us. We need someone to help them understand that we can't allow these so-called owners of the states and cities to push us around. We have the strength we just need someone who understands what it is like to be forced to do something against their will and show the public that they are fighting. We know that Malachi Blackstone threatened you into marriage and Adriana said that you have contacted her about finding a way to make you disappear. Of course, when she told me she didn't know I was representing the organization to see if you were right to be our voice. What do you think? Will you speak for us?" Dear Gods, Mari was talking about the Royals. How did this innocent child get involved with them?

"Mari, this organization, quit it." Rhia urged Mari and she again ignored the anger that flared in Mari's eyes. "They're up to no good. They want destruction and chaos. Get as far away as possible." Mari sighed.

"I was really hoping that I was wrong. It seems we got to you too late." And quickly Mari surged her body, pushing against Rhia with a Xavier dagger clasped in her hand aiming for Rhia's heart. Quick on her feet, Rhia wrapped her hands around the dagger, pushing her knees into her stomach and lifting until Mari flew over her head and behind the couch. Before Rhia could get up, Mari's hand came over her head with the dagger dangerously close to the vein in her neck. Rhia's blood boiled and she bit into Mari's arm. Mari didn't scream, but the dagger dropped from her hand. Rhia picked it up and stood. Mari was circling around the couch until Mari was standing in front of Rhia. Mari's stance was low and her fist clenched tight. Mari jumped and Rhia dodged to the left. Mari's fist swung and connected to the back of Rhia's head. Mari's foot smashed into her knees and pain bound her body, but Rhia kept standing. She had let her guard down because Mari was someone she had taken care of and trusted. Mari's fist smashed into Rhia's stomach and it felt like a pound of bricks. Rhia couldn't breathe, but she wouldn't die. Too many were counting on her. Kai. Lucy. Genny. The entire Blackstone Organization. She was the *Dona* and she could not die here by a child's hand. Rhia didn't plan it.

As she pushed herself up and threw her entire body at Mari, she never once planned it. She forgot about the dagger. As she pulled Mari by her waist, it dug into Mari's side. Coldness. Shadows. A wisp of decayed earth. Blood dripped from Mari's body. Coldness slipped into Mari's skin and the light was leaving Mari's eyes, but Rhia's lungs and heart burned. Lilies, the scent that always seemed wrapped around Mari since she was a child. Rhia breathed it in. She breathed Mari in. A light blue aura that surrounded Mari's body flowed like the wind and she sucked it into her body. Rhia drained Mari of her essence, her very life force was pulled inside of Rhia. And then there was no more Mari. She was dead as Rhia held Mari in her arms shakily. A deep, booming, loud, banging, and powerful voice shouted inside Rhia's head.

Rhia Ambria Rivers: Huntress of the Halden Clan
Marks: 1

Dagger Stained

Song Dedication: Invincible by Ruelle

8.49 AM
Blackstone Manor

The meeting with Tariq and Julian went smoothly. Kai didn't know if they would have been able to work so well without the threat of war over their heads. They had agreed that they would each use a man that they absolutely trust to act as a messenger so that information could not be altered through technology. He simply had to go home and work on battle strategies. At least that was the plan. He came home to total silence. *Madre* and Lucy along with Alek were standing in the living room doorway looking at something. He could tell by the look on *Madre's* face that what they were seeing was upsetting. He found Rhia on her knees in a yellow dress with red dots scrubbing at the carpet, red stains coated the white fur. Blood. He pulled *Madre* aside to see if he could get some answers before talking to Rhia. "What happened?" His tone was not meant to argue. If they had been attacked in their home again, he was going to take a bite out of the guards.

"We don't know. Alek says that she had a visitor. One she seemed happy to see, but he heard crying and when he came in, he found Rhia holding the woman and she was dead. She hasn't talked. Nor did she let May Lin clean up the mess. She insisted on doing it herself." Well damn, he didn't like that scenario one bit.

"Go upstairs. All of you!" Rhia didn't even flinch at his shout, but they moved. Sean and Paul trailed behind his mother and sister. Good. As he entered the living room, the stench of bleach floated to his nose. Rhia had been scrubbing so long that her knuckles were paling. He saw the tears in her eyes, and he wanted to kill the person that had caused her such pain. As he lays his hand on her arm flashes flare inside his mind and he knew exactly what had happened. This was worse than when he killed Maya slowly. Like him, this was something Rhia must face on her own. He sat down on the couch and waited. He watched her as she dumped the towel in the bleach fill bucket, wrung the towel out, and scrubbed against the blood stains. That wouldn't bring out the blood stains, but until she became frustrated, that was what he would allow her to do. He watched as she repeated this process. He lost count of how many times she repeated it. Finally, she screamed. Tears burning tracks down her face, and cracks splintering her soul, she screamed. She swung the towel, throwing it away and the bucket of bleach spilled. When she was done, she stood, and her eyes were a very light purple.

"Around this time I would be teaching Lucy how to fight, but I... I can't. Too much pain... a... a... an... and rage is surging through me. Will... will... will you spare with me?" Right this second, she needed a battle. Something to help release her pain and anger. He didn't respond to her question. He made his way up the stairs and to their room. Rhia followed and she knew that he had agreed. After she found her clothes, she changed right there with the door nearly halfway open. This death had unhinged her more than the Jang brothers. Possibly because this was someone who had held a piece of her heart. Or more because the hunt had forced her to take another soul. Even he couldn't understand what that meant. They would need to track down her father to get her some training. Otherwise, this may happen again. She put on black tights and a black tank. Inside the training room, he noticed that the purple of her eyes had become deeper. Darker. Almost the same shade as when she had a panic attack and blindly attacked. As he moved into his stance, she was already moving. Flying into the air. Flipping with her left leg straight out. Her foot kicked into the back of his right shoulder blade and that power was back. Filled with energy, strength and rage she pressed until his knee hit the floor. Before she could jump back, he wrapped his hands around her ankle and twisted her to the ground. He grappled, trying to hold on to her. She locked her ankles around his head, cutting off his airway. He gasped. Pushing at the soles of his feet, he pushed them to a stand. Then he grabbed her thighs and flipped them. Her ankles unlocked as they fall, immediately she kicked him in the face.

With his hands balancing him, he spun his legs high and connected to her stomach, pushing her away from him. He pushed to a stance and as she caught her breath, she looked up. The deep purple was spiraling into pitch black. He tackled her before she could change tactics. They slammed into the far wall. With her middle finger farther out than the rest of her fingers, she punched at his lower face, near his ear. Sound boomed and faded. The bare crackle of their air rasping out shook into his ears. Balling a tight fist, he hit her square in the chest. Her back hit the wall and she arched. She shook her head and glared up at him. Hunter-green was filling her entire eyes. So, this was how that color came to be. He didn't see her. She just moved low. Kicking at his chest, pushing her hands on his shoulders and flipping over him. Then she wrapped her entire body around him. Blows hit the back of his head. There was once a time that this would cause him severe pain – instead he found delight and joy at her plan. Spinning and slamming her against the wall she slipped from around his waist. He spun and came face to face with a Xavier dagger stained in blood. He knew this was the one she used on Mari. He eased back. Although he knew that Rhia didn't want to hurt him, the sparing circle now had new taste. Rhia wanted to hurt herself, but she needed someone who wouldn't take too kindly to the use of knives and the authority to keep fighting her. That made him the only available person. As she lunged at him, he swiped the dagger and tossed it across the room. He nipped himself at the edge, drawing blood. He pinned her to the floor. Not even seeing him, she wrangled, trying to escape.

"Rhia." He called to her. Violet orbs stared back at him. Not understanding or even human. "Huntress…" he whispered and she stopped moving. "There is no hunt here. Only pain and grief to be met. Go back." Silently those orbs focused on him. Judging him but listening, and slowly the color faded. Orbs of violet purple. Hollow, pitch-black eyes. Dark purple. Light purple. White orbs. And then, her beautiful hunter-green eyes flared back in. He wanted to touch her. To comfort her. Make everything right, but he couldn't. Nothing but Rhia's acceptance could make this okay.

"Mari's essence lives in the dagger. It shall always be stained red and only I can weld it. It would kill any other who tries." He didn't even question how she knew that. Damned voices that come and go probably told her. However, he understood what she wasn't saying. If the dagger held Mari's essence, then Mari's soul couldn't move on to be reborn until Rhia dies. "That is what a *mark* is. Souls that can't be redeemed in the crossover time. They must make penance at my hands. Life for sins. Service in the weapons that end them until I end in this life." Tears formed at the edge of her eyes. "I don't want to have any *marks*, Kai. Not if it means trapping souls." Silently she cried, pinned under him to floor. One of the most powerful persons he had ever come to meet. He understood why her clan needed anchors, then. The weight of the gift must take on their minds and make them wish to end it all. Her clan must have experienced times where they considered suicide. Anchors. Anchors will always pull them back up. Even when they don't wish to. After all the unredeemed will need second chances. And only the hunters seem to have the ability to balance those chances.

Ranks

Song Dedication: Sing by My Chemical Romance

Kai was unstrapping the bands from her hands. Rhia had to admit that allowing him to see the fragility of her heart wasn't easy though she had come to trust him. "I need to call an organized meeting." Rhia thought she breathed easier when he spoke. Then she didn't have to make the first move. In a way that made her more of a coward. She sipped on the water that Kai had handed her. "That means that anyone apart of the Blackstone Family will need to attend." The elders and all. That was a lot of people. In Bossier City alone it was at least six hundred members. Not to mention the ones in the other states.

"Why?" She would never know everyone that was in their organization, but she should understand the reason by making such a call. In case it happened again.

"War is coming. The ranks need to be reestablished. And we need to name our right and left hands." Accepting her new life had been easier than she first thought it would be. Adjusting to her powers would hinder her. And she blamed this war. For now, the Royals were pacing themselves. Hitting at smaller points. Kai saw there was a bigger attack coming and he wasn't waiting any more.

"What are they? Right and left hands?" He was unstrapping the bands from his own hands. She popped her fingers in nervous habit. One in which she had not used in years.

"When you go down and can't get up for a while, they represent you. Your right hand is your voice. They speak for you. Your left hand is your trigger. They act on your command as a hidden weapon." A voice and a weapon. In the struggle for power, it was understandable to have one, yet she could see the risk in taking one that you didn't have complete trust in. "We both need them. It is the written rule. That way if something terrible happens, we are both covered. The legacy must live." Shockingly, she hadn't been looking at it like that. Until they had a named heir, they were the legacy of the Blackstone Family.

"So, Sean and Paul must be the ones you'll pick as hands. That leaves only me." As she gave his legs a soft massage, a grimace contorted his features, and it wasn't because of the pressure she was putting on him. "Or not." Out of all the guards that lived with them, Sean and Paul were who he trusted the most. If not them, then they had more problems when they made their announcements at the meeting.

"I need Paul to act as my messenger. If this alliance between Alexander, Francesco, and myself is to work, we need our most trusted people to pass on messages, information, and material. To keep us connected." Rhia nodded her head in understanding, but now who the hell would stand as his other hand? Unlike Francesco and Alexander, they had more *family* members to protect, so their risk in this war was more. "Besides Alek, is there anyone else that you trust to act as your left hand?" He believed that she had decided on Alek as her right. He would be wrong.

"Kai, Alek isn't a speaker. Yeah, he is going to be one of my hands, but he suits the left-hand position better, besides, I..." Her vision clouded and glazed. Short flaring red hair. Sea-blue eyes. White caucasian skin. Butterfly birthmark on the inner elbow. "I think I have yet to meet my right hand. Now she knows how to speak," she finished off. In that split second, Rhia saw the person that would never betray her. Also, she was here for more than to be Rhia's voice.

"She?" Kai sounded and looked bewildered at her. She didn't understand, although she hadn't named her right hand what was wrong. "Rhia there has never been a female right hand or left hand. Not in all the history of Blackstone Family." She almost laughed. People always thought that women were the weaker link of the species. So, of course, only men had been named. Women were possibly more dangerous than men.

Then history shall have a new beginning. The new era of the Blackstone's. It was becoming easier to share their thoughts. It was just that they would have to adjust and choose when the best time to use the mind link is. They wouldn't want their enemies aware of such ability.

6.11 PM

For dinner she had cooked Alfredo pasta, white sauce with shredded bits of American cheese, parmesan, rose bread toasted with butter, Italian salad with original ranch dressing, and white wine. Currently, the more deeply inner family members sat at the table enjoying the meal she had cooked. "Bry, could you pass down the salad," Lucy asked cheerfully with a million-watt smile. Although Rhia didn't want to, she froze at the nickname she hadn't heard in a long time. Mari started calling her that when she was younger. She didn't think Rhia suited her and Ambria was a mouthful. So, she had shortened it to Bry. *Lucy, like yourself, hears voices that hand her information. Though probably not as much like yours.* Without sparing a look at her or

Lucy, Kai told her about Lucy's secret in respectful silence. At least to everyone else. She could feel the fact that his family had ignored Lucy's gift from the time it appeared. Not wanting to embarrass Lucy by acknowledging the fact they were more alike than ever, Rhia handed her the bowl of salad.

"*Madre*, I need you to alert the Blackstone members of the Shallow." *Madre* jerked on a small level. Shallow was what they called an organized meeting.

"Of course, *mio filgio*." And for the rest of the night, they tried to fill the moments with happiness Alek, Sean, and Paul would laugh and smile as *Madre* talked about the trouble that her children got her into. It was one of the happiest moments in life. That was when Rhia felt that her family was nearly complete. They were missing something, and she knew that it was only a matter time before they found and completed it.

June 7, 3034
2.30 PM

The Blackstone Organization was huge. They had to go the Eldrighe courts so that they had room. A two-story building with three wide teal windows of glass painting. The Mother of the Sky in her most painful moments depicted in them. The one next to Rhia was of Mother of the Sky sitting in a blue shawl and her son in her arms after he had been taken down from the cross. Tears, stained red, flowed from her eyes as she called upon the High Lord of Heavens to save the son he had gifted her. That one had haunted Rhia from the time she was a child. She didn't pray to anyone, but she always felt as if the Mother was calling her. Waiting and biding her time until Rhia was needed. Rhia thought her time ran out when she saved Kai. And that was the reason why she really didn't want to continue going to Mass on Sundays, but she knew *Madre* wouldn't let her slide again after she finally attended the last time. "Nervous?" Lucy whispered beside her. No, her instincts told her that this meeting was needed. For everything to fall in place we needed this meeting.

"No, but I wish Kai would get started." Rhia tugged at the neck of her sleeveless dark blue turtleneck. Yeah, she knew it was too hot for this shirt but it was decent, not underrated or overrated, with her short black silk skirt that reach just above her knees. She felt so exposed, but Kai said it was perfect. The Organization was family, and she needed to prove that she could be serious in no matter what she wore. More often than not, people noticed the body language rather than the clothes in this business.

Kai's black boots stomped and clomped down the alley. He had gone old world in clothes today, and he looked amazing. A tight, black, short-sleeved shirt that hugged to his body and showed his fit form. Wide, loose, black jeans that gave him room to move, but didn't have anything to hide. Lucy, Alek, and Rhia stood and moved beside him to face the members of the organization. They stood and bowed to the waist in a show of deep respect. Then they sat back down to listen to what Kai had to say. "War is coming. Our enemies are standing in the shadows hiding and sending their weakest members to attack. The ones that are easily discarded. They are not just attacking us, they are attacking our city. The innocents are being harmed in the midst of all this and I refuse to allow this any longer." The crowd was silent. Rhia always believed that although they had to follow their rules, they who ruled states and cities didn't care what happened to them normal folks. Kai was proving her wrong. These men and women whose face showed anger and hate that someone would attack their city and hurt their people were proving her wrong. "So today my wife and I shall name our left and right hands."

Everyone held their breath. "First off, Paul will be working with our allies for me. Therefore, he cannot be one of my hands." There wasn't one face that didn't register shock at the news about Paul. He was taking everything in stride accepting his *Don's* orders. "Sean will be my right hand. And my left hand is..." A tall, brown-haired, black-eyed man stood in the far back. He was almost six foot with flailing arms and thick hands. "Brennan Mackeltar will be my left hand." Rhia wondered if her husband was losing it, because this man didn't look like he could take her down. But then, using her other sight, she could see his auras. White bursting light and a white striped leopard. Heaven help her, he was a sifter. Sifters were humans who were infected with animal DNA during the Campris Wars. The result was they could take on that animal's form. Red and gold caught her eye. Two rows before, the sifter was her right hand. She felt like fate's chain was closing in and locking them.

"Lucy, do you know that girl?" Rhia asked as she lightly pointed out the female.

"Alessandra De Luz, the adopted daughter of the Elders." Switch's daughter. Her aura was cloudy. White and deep-sea blue. Her fair, fragile looks would fool many into thinking she was weak, but she wasn't. This was a woman who had suffered and survived. Alek's breath catches next to Rhia. As she glances over to him his eyes flash black. The only time a Russian eyes flash black is when they see their other half for the first time. When Rhia once fought a Russian in the Blood Rings, his girlfriend came and pleaded for her not to fight him. That was when Rhia learned that Russians, unlike the rest of the world, bond physically to their spouses. Every time Rhia hit him, the girlfriend had felt his pain, and she was pregnant. The stress could harm the baby. That was the only time Rhia walked from a fight. Her last fight to be exact. And she got the Russian out of the rings that night, too. Seems like Alek just met his match.

"Rhia…" Although his voice was soft, she knew he had been trying to get her attention for a while. It was now her turn to make an announcement. Taking a deep breath, Rhia moved to the front.

"I haven't been in the family long. Most of you probably think I'm in over my head and should take a step back." Very few members seemed to disagree. Rhia thought they were the idiots who said everything that comes to their mind. No filter. Especially in front of their *Don*. She couldn't blame them, though. They hadn't seen her in action. More than eighty percent didn't even come to the wedding. So, she understood them. "I won't apologize that I can't do that. My left hand is Alek Alexeev, and my right hand…" Staring directly into the eyes of Jonathan and Alejandro sitting on the front row, she called out, "Alessandra De Luz." Shock slammed into them, and all hell broke loose as voices screamed and shouted in denial.

"Bry…" Rhia turned to Lucy as she called out to her. "Forget them for a sec. What the hell is wrong with your eyes?" And her own life twisted with Lucy's words. History is told. However, before it is told, the story must be lived. And Rhia had enacted a new history. She was creating a new world and Lucy had just pushed herself through. Maybe in that moment, Rhia should have realized the significance that Lucy could see the real her. Sadly, she was too focused on organizing one piece of history that she forgot the other.

Rhia was the daughter of the Halden Clan and she had none. So, fate was lifting the veil and allowing her to create another.

The power of the Hunter Clan was protection. They protected the balance and lost souls. The clan saw the truth and protected them. That is why nothing could be hidden. Yet Rhia didn't see it until it was too late. Why could some who were close to her see and others couldn't? Of course, Rhia didn't know. Not then and not until much later, because she was changing the rules. When you change what a person has lived by for their entire life, you will find an opponent.

Before, as men rose and demanded that she name another, she was working desperately to change the history of women again. Women had been looked down upon and were able to rise up only to be pushed down again. Rhia needed the Blackstone Organization to see that women could fight and win too. Otherwise, it wasn't the war with the Royals that would end them. It would be themselves who couldn't improve and move from the past that would die out, and the Royals would win anyway. Rhia had to remake *history* and restore equality to the broken United Territories. That would prove harder to do than when it first split in the Campris Wars, and she wasn't sure she was ready for politics.

History Remade

Song Dedication: Centuries by Fall Out Boy

Rhia sat down in the chair behind her. She crossed her legs and let the crowd rage and huff. Why waste her breath? "*Don* Kai, I understand she is your wife, but this goes too far. Women are not leaders." And that was her que. Without moving from her chair, she decided to pinpoint their attention to herself rather than everything else around them. Placing her thumb and forefinger between her lips, she lets out a shrill whistle. Many covered their ears as pain registered on their faces.

"Listen to me." She didn't need to shout. She commanded. "You men seem to forget too soon. Women are the reason men are here today. We carry you and bring you into the world. That isn't easy. It takes a lot of strength to do that. And don't discount the women who raise their sons without a father. Many of those men become the greatest leaders. It isn't that women couldn't lead, it is that she has never asked to." Her words were reaching the women sitting down. Since the Campris Wars, they had been repressed and conformed to only certain positions, and what was worse was that they thought that was okay. The thoughts of these women were written on their faces. Although they were not made for strife and leadership, they believed a woman who was tough and intelligent could not truly be a woman. Alessandra stood up from where she had been sitting. The organization turned toward her. Rhia thought that if she had chosen someone who was not an

Elder's daughter then she wouldn't have been able to say as much as she did. Her deep, form-fitting, white, lilac dress was glowing sunshine orange. A new world dress that changed colors to match your mood.

"In the 1920s old world, women won against the State Courts for equality. 2071 New World, Vance Crawford made an unwritten rule while the States were splitting. That rule ensured that not many women owned businesses, worked in high positions, and most importantly owned a territory. I doubt the Royals are adhering to that law. If I wanted to take down my enemies, I would send the people they wouldn't expect to try to harm them. Now they have sent children, that isn't to say they don't have women as leaders." Sucking in a large, deep breath, Alessandra's eyes shone with heat and determination. She had the crowd enraptured, their entire attention on her and what she had to say. Those men that had stood in order to get their point across were now sitting and listening to her. What she was saying was proving that Rhia was right in making Alessandra her voice, and most couldn't disagree with her. "*Dona* Rhia sees that for us to survive and succeed in this war, there needs to be change. Now, I am not saying that I am the right choice for her in some twisted version of power play, but she is right that the women in our organization need to have more active roles. And above all, she is our *Dona*. The only ones who can go against her orders are the *Don* and the Elders. We have no right to speak against her." Her words crashed on them as they realized that by disagreeing with Rhia's choice, they had dishonored the name of the Blackstone organization. Brennan stood before Alessandra could sit.

"I think she has just shown why *Dona* Rhia chose her. Will you stand by the new laws?" He was speaking to the Shallow as a whole. Although he wasn't Kai's voice, it was a show of respect for them both. If any disagreed, they could be cast out. It was phenomenal watching almost two thousand men and women bow to their knees with their arms crossed against them like the letter x. That day, history was made two folded. Alessandra became the first woman as a hand, but more came after her. Her taking the title resulting in female guards, weaponist, and assassins. And that moment was the first act of Rhia's reign as First Queen of Louisiana.

Wearing a modified mask to disguise her looks and using a Wade listening device, Empress really wished Rhia was still on their side. She had just changed history for women across the Territories once again. As a child, Empress thought the only thing Rhia could amount to was being a shut-in freak. The way she always knew things and her empty emotions. The girl used to be a robot, only living day by day, and yet Malachi Blackstone got his hands on her and now the being locked inside had been freed. She was a born *Dona*. And that was rare. *Okay, Rhia Ambria Rivers, you have interfered with Empress plans too many times. Time to stop playing it safe and make things a little harder for yourself. Enjoy these next few days because when they meet again you will wish to never have known Empress.*

A dangerous presence was shadowing Althea's daughter. Their hate and anger which had only simmered was now a burning force. "Daerhae, tell me?" Althea didn't give an exact reason. She didn't know any. She couldn't think as the presence slowly slipped away and still she didn't know who it was. That was worrisome.

"Her past will create her future. She must see past the mask and steel her heart against kindness. Don't worry, my lady. Young Miss Rhia and her clan will survive, and they shall win." Although that soothed some of her nerves, she knew the worst was yet to come. Through Dania's pond, she watched as Rhia walked down between the pews, her people following close behind her, her husband at her side showing a united front, their organization waiting until they were inside, their cars heading back to the Manor before leaving themselves. None slumped down in defeat but boosted up by hope. Yes, maybe Rhia wouldn't come out unscathed, but she would be okay. Althea could only live for that. At least for now, as Althea was trapped in the skies.

First Card of War

Song Dedication: Dance with the devil by Breaking Benjamin

Empress was sitting in her office, Wild Fortress, the company she had complete control of, though her name was not listed as owner. Not for long. She must at least have thanked Rhia for that. The Emerson spy would report to the Emerson family of the new beginning that the Blackstones had made, and would act on it. Sitting in her black, diamond-spotted chair, she looked at her office and imagined the changes. The deep brown high desk, five feet wide and three feet long, could have been traded for a black and red striped low desk. The thick, plain black, no-design curtains could be traded for white and red zigzagged curtains. The awful polka-dotted gold and purple seats could be traded for a nice blue and red. She could uproot the floorboards and install black Germanic glass. She heard that the jewels glowed if someone was carrying a lethal weapon of any kind. Yes, the changes would be nice, despite the cost. Rummaging in her desk, she pulled out a deck of cards. Handmade by the woman she claimed as her grandmother and handed down to her. The tarot cards were personally made for them, and never lied.

"Tell me, Mother Evaryia, who must I send next? Who can help me next to weaken the Blackstones?" She had attacked all three men. She had believed it would be so very easy. However, they formed an alliance and changed everything. United as they were, it was harder to attack them. So, she focused on one and the other two would be easier. Although Blackstone had more power and strength, he was actually the more vulnerable of the three. He had his family. His sister, mother, even those fool-hearted bodyguards he called friends, and now Rhia. Rhia was the unexpected. If not for her, the assassination would have been successful. And then she got entangled and forced into a marriage, thus changing from the weak crazy person Empress thought she was. From the deck, she pulled the wolf dog, barely escaping hell's gate. A smile pulled at her lips. She should have known that he was next. Using the phone lines, she buzzed her secretary in the other room.

"Yes, Empress," her shaky voice came through the line. After she had seen Empress kill a child in cold blood, she was always shaky around Empress. The smart bitch.

"Bring me Elias Santiago." Yes, he would be very useful. For now, at least.

If there was any place El would rather not be, it would be standing in Wild Fortress before Empress's office door. His father used to tell him that his idiotic choices would get him in trouble one day. Going into contractual business with Empress had to be one of the worst decisions he had ever made. He was a Crime Lord. He was okay with the territory he owned, and didn't need any more, but Empress had promised him gold and he had let his greed get the benefit of his instincts. Now he was stuck doing the bidding of a power-hungry psycho maniac who wanted to take back the United Territories. And thanks to the poison, he couldn't just walk away. For the sake of everyone, even he was hoping that Blackstone would succeed in this war. Maybe then he could go rest in death peacefully. He opened the doors and stepped in. She was sitting at her desk in blood red. A cropped bust that tightened around her very large breasts. The dark tan against her skin nearly golden. Black eyes. Pitch black. Almost soulless, and colder than any day he had ever seen them. Blood-red hair streaked with white streaks and white ends. The Blackstones identified the biological children by looking at the red edges, but they forgot that when a child is a naturally born redheaded, then the hair is tinged white. Criminals had standards. They killed. They stole. They owned. They enslaved. They did not attack their family even if they had been abandoned. Empress didn't have those standards. Revenge was a knife twisting in her soul. Cutting against all who came into contact with her. Since the Blackstones hadn't acknowledged her mother and her, therefore leaving them vulnerable to attack, she grew into a being who thought that changing society was the best action. He was all for change, but the way she was going about it was wrong.

"You called for me." It burned his tongue to say those words every single time. It proved that she owned him.

"Yes, I want you to do something for me." Her voice was smooth like white wine. If only the people that worked for her could see past the beguiling smile and charm into the eyes of the devil that she was.

"Name it." Whatever it was couldn't be worse than egging a split between Devon and Malachi. Although he was furious that they hadn't broken, he was also amazed that they had been able to stand by their ethics.

"Kill Rhia Blackstone." Maybe he was wrong. There could be something worse. Empress was trying to get him killed.

They were driving back to the Manor. They had come quite a distance for the Shallow. Rhia had tuned the station to Trizha Bowers, and was leaning against Kai's chest as she let the music flow through her.

> *Wake me to the sunrise*
> *Sunrise*
> *Sunrise*
> *Wake me to the sunlight*
> *Sunlight*
> *Sunlight*
> *Burn me with the sunshine*
> *Sunshine*
> *Sunshine*

My soul that has been coated in darkness is shaking under the light. It flares and flows, burning me from the inside. I come apart. Torn and shaken it rebuilds. Changing who I am. Confusion echoes in my mind and leaves me bewildered. But I'm okay. I went to bed lost and condemned, but now I am redeemed.

> *Wake me to the sunrise*
> *Sunrise*
> *Sunrise*
> *Wake me to the sunlight*
> *Sunlight*
> *Sunlight*
> *Scorch me with the sunlight*
> *Sunlight*
> *Sunlight*

New chances and hope. No more shadows or hidden spaces. I am free. And I shine with the sun.

Kai had to give Trizha credit when it was due. She was good. Her words had a message even with the loud boom, and hypnotic and very distracting bass sounds. Rhia was one of the very few who listened to what she had to say rather than just going along with the bass. "Lucy saw my eyes change color." Normally that would put him on alert, but it was Lucy. "The only people who should be able to see that are ones whose fate aligns with my own."

Taking in her words, something was worrying him, but he couldn't exactly place his finger on it. For now, only a very few could see. Alek, Sean, Lucy, and himself. "Paul, Brennan, and Alessandra saw too. Though they didn't say anything." Inside her mind he saw them stepping outside of Eldrighe Courts. Alessandra had taken a moment to speak to her fathers before leading them out the door. Brennan and Paul had been waiting at the bottom by the autodrives. As she had turned to address Rhia, all three jerked very slightly as their eyes connected with their *Dona's* eyes whose hunter-green orbs were still alive and aware. Yet they tightened their lips and helped her inside the autodrive.

"We have to explain to them once we get to the Manor." Thankfully, Alek and Sean had ridden with them.

"What do you think it means? There must be reason why everyone in that room couldn't see, but they could. Since I am married to you, and the *Dona* of this organization by the laws of natural balance, they should have seen my true self." He kissed the top of her forehead.

"Remember, one moment at a time." There wasn't enough time to question every single thing that came their way. The answers would come when they needed to.

Called Out

Song Dedication: Us Against the World by Westlife

Blackstone Manor

As Kai stepped outside of the car he pointed to Lucy, Brennan, Paul, and Alessandra. "You four – follow us to my office." Rhia helped Lucy to steady herself in her very high, red, criss-cross-tied, heeled boots. Alek and Sean knew what they needed to talk about, so they stayed on the lower floor in case *Madre* needed them. Unlike any other home they owned, his office was on the third floor rather than first floor. For that reason, it was slighter smaller. He was able to have a wide black cotton couch and a black five-by-four desk inside. The walls were coated dark brown and there were black curtains.

He turned on the lights as they entered. So much black made it darker even during the day, but that was the way he wanted it. No one could see inside or outside. He sat in his chair and leaned back. Rhia helped Lucy take a seat at the couch. How she managed to stand until they left was beyond him. Rhia crossed the floor, pushing her way between Paul and Brennan. She sat at the top edge of his desk and crossed her legs at her ankles. He could clearly see the small, black, snap-on, black ankle boots with a two-inch-wide heel. It was the most adventurous outfit that she had ever adorned, but then again, she was wearing it on his behalf. He wasn't sure if he should be proud that she was opening up or toss her his coat to cover her up. It was only last week that he had noticed Rhia dressed by how much she trusted people and felt safe in the place she was at. Covered from neck to foot, it meant she didn't feel safe anywhere or with anyone. By taking his advice and wearing the short-sleeved turtleneck with the silk black button skirt, she made a statement. She wasn't trusting those that may surround, she was trusting him and her guards with her safety. And she was beginning to trust herself.

"I'm sure you have questions, so ask." Rhia's eyes were back to their normal hunter-green. Maybe that was why they hesitated, and Lucy had to take the first leap.

"Back at Eldrighe, your eyes were *pure* green." It wasn't a question, but you could almost hear what Lucy wanted to ask.

"You can blame the Campris Wars. What I have been able to find out is on my maternal side, the one with my eye color, can change to other colors. Only family members should be able to see. It sometimes gives us warnings." Due to growing up in an orphanage, Rhia didn't have much experience with others seeing her true self. "I am the last of my mother's line. I thought that would be my only gift, but then I started *seeing* things. My eyes weren't just changing colors. I began to see events before they happened. So, Kai took me to have a Neptune's Reading..." She glanced up and faced them all, breathing deeply and accepting that other truth that she had been trying so hard to forget. "I am a True Seer." Alessandra was the only one to understand what that meant.

"What she means is a seer can see possibilities that can't be changed, but a True Seer sees what will come to be and can change what she foresees." The power that a true seer had made them one of the most coveted beings in this time. Thankfully, they were also the rarest living being, which made it harder to find one, but even harder to protect one from being taken against their will.

"That's how I knew to choose you, Alessandra. I saw you when Kai and I were talking about naming our hands." Her shoes tapped against the black stained-glass floor as she walked to her. Holding Alessandra's hands, she said, "Fate, that being who twists everything around us, called you for me. Normally I dislike her interference, but for once she has it right." Lucy sighed into the background, breaking the ice that had been building in the room.

"Can *Madre* see too?" Maybe the similarity between them was the reason everything was going smoothly.

"No, so far besides everyone in this room, Alek and Sean are the only others who can." He crossed his arms and leaned back. Today was going to be long enough as it was. "If there are no more questions, you're dismissed." Moving at a slow pace, the four of them exited the room. He didn't even notice his eyes closing. Rhia's perfume floated under his senses. Awakening his tired eyes even as they pleaded for rest. Although many members would return to the territory they came from, there would be more than a few who would come and seek audience with him. Rhia's tiny finger pushed into his shoulders, hitting the pressure points beautifully.

"I'll make drinks and snacks for any who decides to come." He wanted to smile, but he was too tired. Setting up the Shallow had been keeping him quite busy. "You need a nap. You haven't rested since yesterday. That's over thirty hours without sleep."

Come to bed with me. Even the echo of his voice in their minds was sluggish. Levering himself against Rhia, they began to move to their room. Their steps were slow as they made it down the stairs. *They'll give me an hour at least.* Rhia's memories surfaced. Dozens of men against her wishes. All who wanted what's best for the family.

There will still be a few against my ideas. He opened the bedroom door. Rhia closed it fully and helped him to the bed.

Yes, but together we will make them see. You were right. Change must happen for us to survive. The pillow was a soft welcoming. As he was drifting off, he realized Rhia was standing to leave. Taking her hand, he tugged until she fell in the bed next to him. *You have been awake nearly as long as me. Take a break.* He went to sleep with Rhia in his arms. Even though war was hammering at their doors, it was nice to rest like normal beings.

Rhia woke up first. She could see small sparks of color at their front door in her mind. Must have gone hand in hand with her other inherited abilities. Ones she learned applied to the huntress. Not the True Seer. A true seer was said to see everything that made a person. That was why you couldn't lie to one. She didn't change her clothes, and since Kai had a little time, she left him to get some more rest. She headed down to the kitchen to make snacks for their guests.

"*Madre.*" *Madre* was in the kitchen.

"Ah, sorry to enter your domain…" *Madre* laughed high and joyful. "Sean said you and Kai were asleep. I thought I could make the snacks to give you guys some more time." *Madre* smiled again, but it was dimmer. Since the Campris Wars, there hadn't been a war of this magnitude. The fact that the Blackstone family had been cast in as the catalyst was an unforeseen circumstance. Although Madre wasn't saying anything, she must have wished that this would all end soon.

"*Madre*…" Maybe it was something in her voice, because *Madre* turned away from her.

"I know Markus protected me too much. Maybe it was because of how we started out, but he didn't want me to see the darker side of his life. It has left me ill prepared. That's why I am thankful that fate threw you two together. Fate is funny. She doesn't always act, but when she does it is for the best that you answer her call. It may not look good in the beginning, but it ends with your happiest life." It was the most emotional moment since Rhia started calling her *Madre*. Rhia thought it better that it didn't seem like *Madre* was shedding her personal scars. So, Rhia went to the refrigerator and pulled out cucumbers, carrots, apples, strawberries, and grapes. As she peeled the cucumbers, she could feel the flutter of Kai waking up.

Hello, beautiful. No time to change clothes you have guest. Head to the third floor. Kai still felt tired to her, but not to the point where he was likely to faint. For the rest of the day, she listened in on Kai's meetings using his eyes to *see* the person he was speaking with, giving her own comments on what she believed about their opinion and character, all the while keeping the ones downstairs slightly distracted and not staggering to hunger with the snacks. Alessandra wasn't used to their lifestyle, so she stood beside Alek outside the kitchen door talking. It was a first for her. Alek didn't talk much, but he was helping Alessandra fit into her new role. A few came to congratulate them as they couldn't make it to the wedding. It didn't even feel like such a short amount of time had passed since then. Many came to report the happening in their part of the territory in person. The system was that they mailed the reports to Kai at the end of the month unless there was trouble. A small clutter came to convince Kai that as his wife she was entitled to the name *Dona*, but her active rights should be revoked. They left grumbling. Rhia didn't believe they realized the changes of their roles because of what they had asked for. Kai and Rhia may have been able to make others see this was for the best, but it would have taken too long with a war dragging out.

That is why it shall be temporary, Kai had stated as she saw he planned to have those men demoted.

Won't it make it worse? After all it would be hard to go against what they have become use to.

Others did, but these guys are older. I want to give them time to open their eyes. It was well past midnight when she escorted the last member out. At the door, he bowed at a forty-five-degree angle at the waist.

"Blessing upon the King and Queen."

Ahh! He must be from the Bossier City or Baton Rouge division. Most of Louisiana population were aware of the change of titles that had occurred at the wake. When more than five territory owners had bowed to Kai, they had acknowledged his superiority over them. That was what made a King by the law, even though it had never been acted upon until then. Tariq and Francesco hadn't bowed, so many were wondering if by chance of fate there was more than one King. It would certainly make history.

"Thank you," she said, and gently closed the door. Taking a deep breath, she looked up the stairs to see Kai waiting for her. It seemed that while she was busy, he had dismissed their hands for the night. His fingers curled into her hair, massaging her scalp as they went up the stairs to our room. As the door closed behind them, Kai pulled her close and kissed her as softly as ever before. His lips weren't made to be soft, but he ensured that the kiss was one that left her breathless.

Let's please ourselves tonight. Before her eyes, the entire room was alight. Golden flames flickered from small candles.

White and purple orchid flowers layered the floor and bed. Soft, soothing music was playing. *Are you going for romance?* Untucking her shirt from her skirt, his hand slipped under and ran against her cool skin compared to his heat.

Like it's the last night of our lives. His hands dipped into her panties, his fingers curved up, and a jolt of pleasure surged through her. Her mind short circuited. Her tiny fingers graced and slid against his jeans. She unbuttoned his jeans and the sound of his zipper sliding down was heavier than their breaths. Rhia gasped as he added another finger so that she couldn't sway him. Determination kicked deep within her. She tugged on his jeans, pulling them until at last they flopped to the floor. Kai kept up his pace. Slow and deep. Sending wide ranges of tingles through her. His other hand pinched her nipples lightly, twisting them softly between his fingers. Pulling him closer to her, she softly bit his lower lip so that he opened up for her. As her tongue pushed inside, she got that taste that only seemed to be attached to him. Chocolate covered cherries. Bitter and sweet. Smooth and raw. Desire, lust, and love wrapped into one. He was the beginning of her everything. First kiss. First touch. First burning heat. She felt her skirt fall to the floor. His hands that had been distracting her moved to her waist. Her lace panties caressed her skin as he removed them down her legs. He kissed both her inner thighs. Pulling on his hair strands, she forced him to look up at her.

Tonight I get to please you. And she pulled his shirt over and off. There he was, gloriously naked. There wasn't another man like him. She kissed his tattoo. Sucked lightly on the skin above his bellybutton. Before she could go farther he caught her and spun her around with her back facing him.

For this we shall both be naked. At the barely seen zipper at the back of her turtleneck, he pulled it down, pushing it forward down around her shoulders. His lips left a soft touch against her bare neck as he unsnapped her strapless bra. She turned to him, pushing him down on the bed, and at the edge she fell to her knees and contemplated how exactly this was done. She wanted to please Kai. She wanted them both to enjoy this moment, but she hadn't done this before and Kai was very large. Thick and well-endowed, someone would say. She felt the caress of his hands in her hair and, against her better judgement, she looked into his eyes. Her own filled with curiosity and fear. *First is touch, get a feel of it.* She wrapped her hands around his cock. They couldn't even hold it together as it was. He was warm and much harder than she thought it would feel like in her hands. "Tighter," his deep voice commanded. She tightened her grip and a thick precum escaped. She licked the tip. It was... salty. She sucked the tip as she rolled her tongue around his cock. Slowly she sucked him inch by inch. She couldn't fit the whole of him inside and she wasn't about to try. Judging by the sound he was making, he was enjoying himself anyway. She swirled her tongue around him and pulled gently on his balls. Just as she felt them tighten in preparation for an explosion, Kai commanded, *Enough!* He pulled her up by the arms and caught her up under her thighs, lifting her around his waist. They slammed into the bed. Kai was touching her everywhere. Inflaming her body.

Protection. They kept forgetting, so before they both got lost in the heat, she demanded it.

Don't have it. Next time. He was kissing liquid fire against her breast. Sucking on her nipples. She was shaking and aching.

Kai, next time will be – Without warning he entered her. Her mind splintered, and together they fused, becoming one. She could feel everything. The way her walls tightened around him.

The beating of their hearts. Their pace. Slow, easy, enticing. The flow of passion as it grew higher and higher. Kai hit that wondrous spot, their bodies becoming thunderous, moving faster and faster until light shone and they found completion. Shakes racked her body and quivers raced through her nerves. Kai breathed heavily as he layed gentle kisses against her breast.

That was amazing! She would kill him if she wasn't so damn satisfied. She drifted to sleep in Kai's arms. At least when they slept there was peace.

She woke to someone shaking her arms.

"Madam, phone for you," May Lin's computerized voice floats inside her ears. Her eyes fluttered open and she saw Kai slightly sheepish and hair tousled. He was holding the phone for her. It was not even eight in the morning judging by the clock on the bed stand that she could barely see. "Hello." Her voice croaked at barely a whisper.

"Rhia, thank God!" It was Priscilla, and she sounded both panicked and freaked out. Priscilla's warm deep voice was high enough to break glass. "Look, some woman was just here looking for you. She's scary of a class ten. She shot Thomas." Thomas was the landlord at JT Complex. Priscilla had been moving her stuff out for the last week. Thanks to Kai, Priscilla was able to buy her a house.

"Give me thirty minutes. I'm coming over." Like Rhia, before she got involved with Kai, Priscilla had never witnessed so much violence or death. They were the innocents in this new world. As innocent as they could come in their society.

"Take Sean with you," Kai said as she dug into her drawer for something decent to wear. As much as she would have liked to cover every piece of her skin, people in JT would recognize her instantly. She pulled out a light blue and white striped shirt where the sleeves reach the elbows and black skinny jeans. With her black wedges she could blend right in. After she showered, she tied her shirt a few inches above her bellybutton and she scooped her hair into a side twist that was held by a red scrunchie. It was deadly quiet when the four of them made it to the complex. This place had never been deserted. Not seeing any red tape, Rhia figured Guardians hadn't been called.

"Is it normally this abandoned?" Alessandra asked. No, this was Walker Street. Everything and anyone was cheaper around here. It would be bursting with… business… even at this time of the day. Alek didn't need to be told as he pulled out his Rystic, Sean doing the same. Alessandra was receiving training, so she didn't have a real weapon just yet. Basically, if things went wrong, she was to take Rhia and run. Priscilla opened the door before Rhia knocked.

"Thank God. People are scared." Priscilla being one of them. Priscilla was frazzled still in her silver silk boxer and tank top. "This tall, black-haired lady banged on my door before sunrise. She said she was here to pick up Bry. I was confused until she started describing you. So, I told her you lived with Malachi, your husband. She was so pissed and then Thomas walked in and started making suggestions about your relationship. Said he could take her to you. She took him outside and killed him. Everyone heard it. She dragged his body down the steps and disappeared." Finally, Priscilla seemed to catch her breath. Besides Mari and Lucy, there was one other person that would call Rhia by the name Bry. Priscilla was talking about Adriana. There was also the fact that only she could kill so quickly and knew Rhia. Damn! She forgot to tell Adrianna that she wasn't needing her to save Rhia.

"Okay so no one has called the Guardians." Priscilla shook

her head no. That was great. "Stay inside I will send help for you to move you out. Let's go." They were nearly to the car when they were cut off. El Santiago and a dark beast.

El believed today was the last day that he would be alive. He told his sons that no matter what she dangled before their faces, they were not to sign a contract with Empress. If Malachi Blackstone was going to kill him in an act of revenge for Rhia Blackstone, then he wanted his family safe from the crazy woman. That was if he was successful. If he wasn't, then he shuddered at his own end. 'Papa' Estelle, Noah's wife called to him. It was small even for a yell. He stepped outside his room to find Estelle waiting for him. At five foot four inches El was barely towering over her. She had curled her short brown hair. He was thankful to Estelle because she was able to get Noah to come back to the family. Noah was El's youngest son who had everything that made up his mother. Her soft looks. Her soft manners. Her soft heart. Estelle handed El a note. By the handwriting he could tell it was from Empress.

A gift to help your success. He was confused until he looked up behind Estelle. A large, gray wolf head. Seven feet tall and a body made of bulky muscles. Large fangs. Black orbs for eyes. A dark beast. Sifters that had gotten trapped between their forms. Controlled by the being that had cursed them in between forms. *Oh, damn.*

"Rhia will be at JT Complex apartments. The Empress says hurry." Although his… snout… didn't move, a clear voice had rung out. It was time.

"Tell the boys to do what is best for the family. Nothing more." Estelle's hands twisted in worry, but she didn't try to stop him. JT was close to their vocational home that they had been staying in. As they walked up to Rhia and her gang something seemed off. "The Empress commands your death." The dark beast roared at Rhia. She didn't move an inch, but the other three stepped back just slightly, and that was when El saw it. A bare shimmering light was shadowing Rhia.

Oh, shit. Now was one of the rare times he wished the family gift had skipped him. The dark beast raised his claws to strike since he hadn't moved. *High Lord of Heavens forgive me.* And El threw himself in front of Rhia. His thick claws dug into his skin, scorching his back with pained fire. "Look... a... at... blood... lines." He could feel the dark beast claws as they caught his heart and ripped it from his body. Shock and compassion on Rhia's face was the last he saw before his eternal sleep. A soft hum of Gaelic Warriors' homecoming the last sound to soothe his spirit.

Kai was in his office reviewing the reports when emotions bombarded him. Anger, hate, pain, a gentle wish for peace, and Rhia's soft voice screaming as if the Heavens were falling. *Kai.* Her wail pierced his eardrums like a volcano rupturing. He could see them, kneeled to the ground prepared to face a dark beast.

No! He called on something that he had denied having since he first killed. That dark twisted energy was roused and spiraling outside of his being. It circled. Bound. Locked. Surged up and protected his people. A fortress of seven dimensional walls five elements deep. As the beast rammed into the wall the energy wrapped itself in chains. Locking, shaking. Grower smaller and smaller until only a man sat bawled up and catching a breath. His secret had been called and commanded. He tamed the wild. In men and beast. The darkest and most dangerous power since the wars.

Rhia...!

Secrets Unveiled

Song Dedication: Rescue Me by Kerrie Roberts

In those last seconds, Rhia really thought she would die. She had heard many stories about people who had near death experiences, and they said their lives flash in the mind like a short film movie. Some saw the happiest moment or biggest regret. Others saw their last I-love-yous and goodbyes to their loved one. She froze. For so long she was just moving but not really moving. There were no happy moments or even regrets. She even thought to herself if there was anyone in this world that she really loved enough to remember as she faced death. Then a small light glowed in her darkness. Kai. His smile. His laugh. His glare. How serious he always was. His determination to do what was best for the family. The way he touched her. How he could light the fire of her soul. How comfortable and open she was with him. Kai, the man she said she loved and yet until this moment she didn't think that was really true. Maybe it was the realization that made fate and the heavens changed their decision.

As the dark beast charged at her suddenly, El Santiago surged forward and took the hit for her. In his eyes she saw a plea for forgiveness and relief that he was free along with determination. "L... Look... at... blood... lines." As his last words escaped him in a strong desire to make him feel at peace, a song as old as time itself sung from her soul. Warriors chanting as they adopted an outsider and brought him home. All was not over yet. The dark beast raised his bloody claws once more.

Kai! She called to him. She screamed until distance was but an inch. In her mind, near their bond, she saw Kai standing. Fear and anger placated his features and then she felt it. The flare of dark power. It coated his aura in silver and black swarming before his head. It materialized from a small wolf into a great white dragon with piercing blue eyes filled with knowledge and a sense of ancient power. The dragon gazed at her. Judged her. Seeing all her secrets and then taking those secrets as its own. Accepting her. Pulling them in tighter bond. More than two. Less than three. The dragon arched and flew across the threads of their bond. Flowing within her, but not a part of her. His sharp fangs rasped again the air and a small force field surrounded them. Protecting them from the dark beast. Yet the beast was unable to go against the command of his master. Fluttering like a butterfly wing, the dragon grasped that knowledge from her mind.

It has been a long time since I faced one such as itself, and he opened his mouth, throwing out a wild electric bolt. As the beast charged and hit the force field, the bolts grasped the dark beast tangling in a desperate fight. Over winning the creature and chaining in. Pushing until the creature bent to its true will. To the will of the man that made it sifter and free, therefore leaving a naked and shaking man at their feet. Throughout it all, Rhia realized what this dragon from Kai was, and she knew that she alone knew this secret. Not even those who held the ability were aware of it. Tamers were just higher-powered sifters. Tamers were the peacekeepers and balance-makers of the shadow marked and those who were seen as normal. That was why their power was seen as dark. Tamers could give or take gifts from the twisted unnatural people that begun to rise after the Campris Wars. And her husband had locked his away deep within himself in fear of what that power would do. *You must make him see. The both of you need me during this war. You more than himself. I must not be caged again.* And Rhia swore that no matter what it would take that she would ensure this being stayed free to protect their family. No matter what she had to lose, she would protect those that she saw belonging to her and the man she loves.

Empress watched her beast be freed. Anger like the flames of hell flared inside her heart. How dare she! Rhia had no right to free her creature. Rhia had no right to lift her power over anyone. Empress wanted to rage. To strike out. To destroy. To maim and kill. That would be costly. Rhia, Empress was beginning to see, was a more powerful enemy that she wished for. It was not an advantage to her if Rhia was standing on the opposite. Then she needed to get Rhia to come to her side. That, however, would not happen so long as Rhia fancied herself in love with Malachi. No – if Empress wanted Rhia, then the bond between them needed to be broken. "I don't care how much it will cost me, find me someone with enough power to splinter Malachi and Rhia. A sigyeil or any shadow mark should have something to help me. I want it done. And I MEAN NOW!" Empress commanded her trusted servant Brutus. Too many times had her plans gone awry. She thought that by killing Rhia everything would work out. Empress sees now she was wrong.

As Rhia came closer to the manor, the more on edge Kai became. He had not sent men after her. He had seen that she was safe and had to figure a way to handle Santiago. Kai had sent a team out to take his body to his family. For some reason, El had saved Rhia and, as eternal thanks, his family was now forever under Kai's protection. He highly doubted that was what they should want in the end. He couldn't help but think that now that his secret was out, Rhia would be furious. After all, she believed that only she and Lucy had been touched by the meteor bombing. Although the Campris Wars had well passed over, the altered DNA in people could never be changed, just passed on. He remembered telling her his family would make her look like a fool. In the end it was he who had made her a fool. Could she ever forgive him?

He heard the door shut and that flowing energy was returned to him. Bouncing with joy and happiness. Relieved to be released and a high range of desire to see to Rhia's every need and want. That was conflicting. It had never felt so alive. And he had a feeling that it would never be silenced again. Rhia stepped into their room. There was blood all over her. "I'll bring you your clothes. Go hop in the shower." He could imagine after that morning events that she wouldn't be leaving the manor any time soon. Rhia was washing the blood from her hair when he walked in. "So... about my gift..." Before he could say more, she stepped out and wrapped a towel around her.

"It is a weapon. Learn to use it." He didn't know what shocked him more that she was okay with it or the fact that on a small level he agreed with her. "Did you figure out what Elias' last words meant?" If he didn't know better, he would swear she was doing it on purpose. Being so nonchalant about everything.

"The message is obvious. Bloodlines. The question is whose. When Santiago passed on the information, he must have believed we would understand it. Yet I can't figure out whose bloodline he spoke of." In these circumstances it could have been anyone.

"Then we must do everything we can to figure out which bloodline. I think our enemy's identity lies in that secret."

Kai had told Genny about the message that Santiago had left. Bloodlines. Bloodlines. Like a witch's chanting, it shouted in her mind over and over again. Memories surfaced. Long dead and pushed into a corner.

Twenty-six years ago
Blackstone Sanctuary
Tampa, Florida

Kai was playing with the guns again. No matter how many times she told that boy no, she could not hide them, he somehow always found them and would play that ridiculous game that young heirs played where they take weapons apart. Most tried to beat their previous time the game was called how many seconds. It was his father's fault that he played such a game. What other normal child would find enjoyment in taking apart a gun and putting it back together in less than a minute? Not to mention the chemicals in the bullets could have horrid effects. When Markus got back, Genny was going to kill him. She understood teaching their son to be strong, but this was just plain crazy. The door slammed and echoed all the way outside. "Markus…" He hardly ever got mad enough to do damage. In the living room, her husband paced the floor. His fingertips bunched his hair in his hands. "Markus…" she called to him softly. He glanced up with eyes blazing in heat and anger. Markus was in a rage. "What's wrong?" His laughter was tinged with hysteria.

"My baby brother is a father. Vane got a *Cacciatrice* that has been cast out pregnant. With none of us the wiser." He picked up the nearest vase and threw it against the wall. It crashed and shattered into a hundred pieces. The chippered ends hit the floor and sounding like rain hitting a tin roof. "It could throw the feud back onto us." *Cacciatrice,* even if she had been out-clanned, she was still their blood, and their families had never gotten along. *Vane, what were you thinking?*

"What shall you do?" She had an idea, and she hoped dearly that she was wrong.

"Nothing else I can do. By our laws, Vane shall not receive any help from the Blackstone Family. That is the only way to keep the peace. Geneva, bring me the Book of Blood." Pain stabbed at her heart. Vane, the youngest of the Blackstone's, had managed to grow without blood stains on his hand. He was all smiles and childlike care. And after that day, she would never be allowed to speak to him or his legacy. In the shed, she pulled the book from its hidden latch. Three feet long and ten inches thick. Gray and blue. Black thorn vines expanding before the picture of the white ice dragon with cold blue eyes, and black-furred wolf with warm, glowing, golden eyes. The Book of Blood. Volvikov etched in blood by the first leader who had risen from the ashes of the Campris War and manhandled control of Shreveport. That dark day, she watched as Markus added the name of Vane's kin and then marked each with a blue jaybird. The jaybird was one of the animals that didn't survive the Wars. It no longer existed and in the book that means Vane was as good as dead to the family.

Twenty-six years later
Blackstone Manor

That memory had circled Genny's mind since Kai told her the message. No longer able to keep it in, she went down to the shed. In the back area in a small corner, she pressed her palm to the floor. A prick of her finger and her blood flowed, activating to release the floorboards. The Book was handed from mother-in-law to daughter-in-law. No true blooded Blackstone had access to it. The events of late had proven that it was time to hand it down, but first, opening the book, she came across the current family.

Vane – Son of Maverick Blackstone, Head of the Family, Only son of Thaddeus.

Married to Caitlyn Meridian – daughter of Khale, leader of Cacciatrice.

Father of Rosadina – born March 3007 dark blood red hair, pitch black eyes, Human.

Genny placed the book back in the ground. Her heart pained again. It was shame that the sins of a father were passed down to a child. A girl. Rosadina. Maybe it was time to find her. To see how Rosadina grew up into womanhood. The heat beat on the back of Genny's head. The sun was high today, yet dark clouds were flowing in. Maybe by some miracle she was wrong. Genny hoped that her suspension would come to naught. "Hello, auntie." That voice chilled her to the bone. Not because of who Genny thought she was and how she got in. That voice itself was colder than ice. Freezing like Alaska waters. Ice glaciers breathing undercurrents with her voice. Genny turned to see a beauty. Nicely formed body. Tall. Nearly six feet. Long red strands of hair flowed to her waist. Eyes as black as the night without the stars. And Genny knew she was wrong. This woman was their enemy. And a cold-blooded killer. Before Genny could sound the alarm, Rosadina sprinkled dust into her eyes. Genny didn't understand at first, but then she choked. Air locked in her throat. Her veins, inflamed, tried to push out of her skin. Darkened and tinged purple. Moon Cave. *Dear Gods.* "Sorry, but I really need you out of the way for the next mission. By the time you awake, the Blackstone shall be no more." And Rosadina walked away with soft laughter. Mother of the sky protect her loved ones. In the far corner of her sight, she could see her children, all three of them racing toward her, and she crashed to ground in a heap of rest.

High in the sky, fear consumed Althea's body. "That disastrous child lived?"

Family

Song Dedication: White Castle, covered by Whitney Woerz

Although Rhia was almost positive Elias Santiago's last words did not refer to her, she couldn't take the chance. So, for the last few days, she had researched her family. Her father's family were called the Hunter's Clan, yet there was nothing on that or the Halden family. Thinking she could find the answer among her mother's history, Kai had told her that he had people looking into her past because of her powers. Yet nearly every last one had come to a loose end. That was easy to see why. Like Blackstone was not his true name, the same seemed to apply for both sides of her family. On her maternal side they went by Ashurwin, and thanks to her aunt she had access to electronic records of Genetic Graphing.co, a website that many families used in today's time to keep track of their blood. She had never used her account since her aunt created it to learn her family history. What would be the point? They would still be dead and she the last descendant. Except for the last hour, she had come to realize that her maternal family had an extensive amount of enemies. It was astonishing to see the numbers, but the shock came from the history of a long-standing feud with a family they called Shikaaree. The feud went even farther back than the Campris War. Way back into AD and apparently originated in Greece not India or Scotland.

Memoir of Dakshayani, the first castor
The long living have named themselves as Gods. It is wrong

and they must be punished. Yet we are not as powerful as them or their pets Shikaaree, the blessed one. Can they not see it is wrong to use the short lives of mortals as entertainment?

790 month of Ares

The long living have gone too far. They have convinced the short-living mortals to build temples in honor of their new titles. Fearful, I have pleaded with the Mother to help us. We are useless unless we may discover a weakness amidst them. The Mother whispered on the wind to wait for she has a plan. I don't know how long we can wait. The mortals have decided the best way to please their 'Gods' is by sacrifice and blood.

790 months of Hades

We battle the Shikaaree each morning and at night we mourn the dead. I lost my youngest daughter today. Though she already saw her death. The gift that the Mother has blessed us with now becomes a curse as more daughters take the pain of the lost. I fear I shall disappoint the Mother, as the fight drains from me with her death. I have lost all hope. My husband. My sons. My daughter. Yet my mother tells me to go on. It was the purpose of Shikaaree and Rakshak to keep the balance. To share the light and the dark. To hold the peace between the long living and mortals. To punish the wicked. Something went wrong with the Shikaaree, and so long as they fight for the long living we cannot win.

790 months of Hera

The winter cold blew in a truth I never considered. She who is now named Aphrodite came to me. She tells me the one called Zeus poisoned many of the Shikaaree. Even if they wished to stand beside us they could not, for their mortal children would die. After talking with the Mother, her anger raged the seas and swarmed the clouds over Atlantis. She called upon the Ancients for her debt to be paid. Hearing her plea they answered. The 'Gods' of Atlantis have been cursed to the Sky above the clouds. In a stasis of movement and near time. In retaliation Zeus called the Shikaaree to the clouds as Sentinels. Only a few escaped.

791 months of Zeus

The Mother has cried and burned the earth. The fire of her heart touching all of us. And with her last breath left us a salvation. A child of the blood three shall free everything. The Blood of a God, the blood of a Shikaaree, and the Blood of a Rakshak. One with these blood ties shall free their ancestor trapped under earth and Atlantis shall fall back to the sea and the so-called Gods shall flow freely within their own chosen clan marking them a demi-God and making the Gods one with the mortals.

791 months of Poseidon

With the death of the Mother, my sisters search for the Shikaaree living on the Earth. I heard them speak of trapping one in order to make the prophecy true. Knowing this is the wrong way to go about this, I in turn have cursed my sisters. To them, the Shikaaree are our enemies, and so only the Head Daughter shall know the truth. I bound our books of history in blood that only she who leads our family shall know the truth until the prophecy has been acted.

After reading this she saw no point of the records. There were no more descendants outside herself. Going to the family tree, she wondered if her father was listed. Maybe there was more that could be found with him.

There she was. More truth than she was prepared for. Ashlynn Mahajan Ashurwin crested with Ethan Dane-Shikaaree and born Rhia Ambria Dakshayani RiverBlood. If that was not enough of a shock, she was not the last living descendant. She had cousins, still alive if the tree was to go by.

Eleanor Mahajan Ashurwin crested with Gabriel Thornton-Human, not shadow-marked and born Lily Aria Devasree Thornton, crested with Thomas Blackwell-Human, shadow-marked and born Theresa Cassandra Aya Dulari Blackwell. Her mother's eldest sister had one daughter before her and another just one month after she was born.

She had family left. Sitting on the bed with the notepad in her hand, she reread the family tree. Embry never mentioned cousins or another older sister. Did she even know where Rhia's cousins were before her death? Maybe like Rhia they had been cast away. Never to be seen. Excitement built in her blood, and she decided if she got the chance after this war ended, she would find them. Yet confusion clouded her thoughts. She should have learned all of this during her Neptune's Reading. No one knew where the technology had exactly come from, but it was supposed to know everything about a person the minute it had their blood. As she was pondering this, the flashes crept in. *Madre* leaving the house. A redheaded woman standing by the door waiting for her. Pain. Realization. Fear. She knew she had only a minute at most. She raced out the room calling Kai, Lucy. Anyone who was closer. At the bottom of the stairs as she spins to take the back door Kai catches her arm. Lucy was standing behind him watching her as she panicked before them.

"Baby, what's wrong?" The endearment flew right over her head. Air broke from her body and in her soul she knew they were too late.

"Danger. *Madre*. Outside." She pressed deep into her lungs to obtain the air so that those few words may escape. Kai pushed off, running to the door. Lucy followed a step behind her as she ran after him. There *Madre* lay on the ground. Dark purple veins raised against her skin. Poisoned. Kai barely touched her. The mystery lady was nowhere in sight.

"Someone call a damn medic. Now!" Kai screamed as he knelt beside *Madre*. They all fell to their knees, staying beside her, telling her to live, and sending a thousand and one prayers to the Mother of the Sky. If *Madre* ever made it past this, she would know she had done one thing in Rhia's life. She made Rhia believe. Believe in Catholicism. Believe in the Mother. And with the strength of that Belief, Rhia prayed that the Mother would not take any more family from her.

The Sound of War

Song Dedication: This is War by 30 Seconds to Mars

Blackstone Manor
July 17, 3034

The drums were sounding.
Boom
Boom
Bam
Beat

Since *Madre* had been in the hospital, the pounding of drums has sounded in Rhia's ear. Softly yet steadily growing louder. Now even the rushing sounds of the stormy sea could not battle the drums. And only she could hear it. It was giving her the headache of the fucking year. As she rubbed her temples, she saw cases being brought inside. More weapons. Since the attack on *Madre*, Kai had taken precautions to the highest authority. Every new-born security and weaponist-designed device had been ordered for the three houses. Their home, Tariq's quarters, and Julian Francesco's dwelling. They had passed messages between the three for the last month. With Kai listed as King of Louisiana, they were gearing up for war. Rhia was nearly positive that each organization had grown in numbers.

Boom
Boom
Bam

Beat
Slam

The more cases she saw come in, the louder the drums got. She needed to speak to Kai. Blood had stained their walls enough, and with drums ringing in her ears, she knew this was nowhere near the end. War was here. And peace was blackened. Colorless. Darkness. Cold. Stars away from Louisiana. Her fingertips pressed into her skull, trying desperately to drive the pain away. Her eyes glazed and gargoyles flew low in her sight. She blinked and the gargoyles were gone as if never there. Instead, Evan stood before her. Evan was the sifter who had been trapped as a dark beast for seven years. In thanks of saving him, he had pledged loyalty to Kai and Rhia. To protect them with his dying breath. She wished he had some memory from being a dark beast – then maybe he could save them the trouble.

Boom
Boom
Bam
Beat
Slam
Pow

He was holding a simpering glass of pink colored water. "You look like you could use this." The strong smell told her it was a medicinal herb. His gold eyes glanced at her. Wolf eyes. Warm eyes. Gray small smooth wings. Blinking fast, the image left. She was losing her mind. And there was nothing anyone could do to help her. The past week, images had pushed into her mind. Messing and scattering her thoughts. And it was not her true sight playing around. She drank the medicine. Sleepiness dragged her body under.

Boom

Boom
Bam
Beat
Slam
Pow
Punch
Bam

"Tell Kai that when he has time to see me in our room, we need to talk." And as if every step pained her, she went back up the stairs. She flopped on the bed. Energy escaped her. And sleeps pulled her in.

Huntress, come thee to me. I call thee. I command thee. Come. Her dreams spiralled and spun, circling in distress. Beige blocks. Tall oak tree. Gargoyles. Pointed lights. Streets signs. Texas. Heat. Burning. Fire. Death. Chains. Destiny. Fate. Duty. Cold. Cold. Cold. Shaking. Someone was shaking her. She came up gasping for air and pulling on the covers. "You're freezing." She heard Kai's voice coming from the closet. He came out with multiple quilts and she didn't have enough breath to thank him. So, she just bundled in the warmth. The shades had darkened. How long had she been asleep? "Hours, you were fighting in your sleep. Wanna talk about it?" As she opened up to talk to him about the weirdness that had plague her, she couldn't remember it. Her mind blanked, the images gone except for the knowledge that she had seen something. Her heart rattled and pained. There was something important. She shook her head rather than admit that she was going insane. Kai looked at her. She could tell he knew something was wrong, but he is all for waiting it out.

"I want to talk to you. About the war." Her lips cracked and broke. They were dry. Too dry – like she was severely dehydrated.

"Before we get into that, I have news. I managed to locate some property in your father's name. In the Dust Fields." That was a step. Since discovering she had more family out there, Rhia guessed she had closed the ties with her father off. Between going to the hospital and seeing *Madre,* she had gone through extreme lengths to find her maternal cousins. Records showed that there were no other bloodlines on her paternal side.

"Where?" It hurt to speak. Gods, she was freezing outside but burning inside.

"Moorisan Dane, House of Daven Dane. Leader and owner of the Dust Fields." The confusion must have shown on her face.

"The Dust Fields wasn't always neutral. In 2483, Daven Dane beat Bryan Westmore and took control of the territory and made it neutral. For years a Sealgair Mor has ruled until Ethan Dane who passed fifteen years ago without a named heir." No heir but an unknown daughter.

"I wish to go there." She choked on her words and tried to stand. Kai pushed her back down.

"Not in this condition," he commanded. She knew he was worried. In the few months he had known her, she had never been so weak. However, she needed to go there. An ache built in her chest. Her heart rate slowed and she could barely keep her eyes open. White eyes. Short blond spiked hair. Something was calling her. She had to go. "Fine." His lips firm, he lifted her up, bridal-style, and her fragile state showed as she was more grateful than angered that he thought she needed help. The Dust Fields had not changed. Still broken and torn. Shattered, but a shattered beauty. The darkness of the Dust Fields, the graying sky that was always there made it into a light beauty. The best place for information was the Savage. It was a bar. Red and black stools. Golden-lined windows, tinted so that you couldn't see inside. Brennan rang the bell hanging outside. A large man stepped out. Three hundred pounds with a huge mass of muscle. Caucasian. Bald. Very light green eyes. Kai was barely able to help her stay still and standing. So, she almost missed the huge phoenix tattoo on his head.

"We're closed. Come back in a few hours." She could hear the tiredness and frustration in him. Her heart chugged and slugged. The rhythm was off. Air was becoming harder to take in.

"One problem with that, Mister. If you don't help us, I might die, and the Danes will really be extinct." Yeah, she wasn't sure about the dying part, but damn if she didn't feel as if she was. He stopped, turns and stared at her. Then dropped to his knees.

"I sincerely apologize, Madam Dane. We thought it would be longer before you came back." He opened the door for them to enter. She was tripping over her feet, the feeling in them gone. "I'll get Howard." She had no idea who this Howard was, but she hoped he was useful. She had minutes, she thought. Kai cupped her hands and breathed on them. His warm breath felt like fire on them. She didn't realize how cold she really was.

"Darling, for your skin color you sure are pale, and not to mention freezing." It was obvious that he made the joke to cover his worry.

"You are most definitely Ethan's girl." How such a soft voice could seem so loud escaped her mind. She looked up, searching for the newcomer. Then around. Twist and spin. "Down here, sweetie." Glancing down, she saw a little man. Around three feet tall with a small round belly. Wood brown hair. Cocoa brown skin. Warm caramel eyes.

"Howard?" Howard did not fit the name of this guy.

"Yours truly." He stared at her hard. Taking in all of her.

"Knew you were a Dane the minute you went to the Old Cave." He saw her last time. Right. The Old Cave and the Savage were right across the street. "Other than your height you a splinting image of Dane. Especially the eyes." Now she was confused.

"My eyes are from my maternal family. Green eyes have been passed down for generations." Aunt Embry had said only green-eyed daughters inherited the gift. Howard's laughter bounced against the walls.

"With that color. Did she specifically say that hunter green eyes were her family gene? Did your mother say that?" No, Aunt Embry never said that hunter green eyes were a trait. Embry said green eyes and her mind made up that unique eye color as normal. "Hunter eyes, we call it. All the Dane Sealgair Mor's had them. You got questions, ask." He placed his hands in his gray pants, leaning back to get a better view of her.

"Where is the House of Dane?" Raspy was her voice. Sluggish. Tired. She leaned into Kai standing behind her.

"Right around the corner. You came to see Anya?" Anya. *Who?*

Huntress, come to me. I call thee. That strange melodic voice hammered inside her brain and the drums roll again. Rubbing at her temples and scrunching her eyes, she asked him to show them the way and come face to face with her insanity. Beige rectangle blocks made the house. Tall oak trees. Dark green, fresh and thriving grass. Deep brown benches. High on top the building large gargoyles that didn't seem to fit. And a large fountain in the center.

Boom
Boom
Bam
Beat

Slam
Punch
Pow
Bam, Bam, Bam, Bam, Bam

The drums drilled inside her mind and Rhia dropped to her knees before the fountain. A statue was before her. A woman in a silver and red cloak. Short blond spiked hair. Small gray wings on her back. White eyes. *Oh, Heavenly Mother of the Sky.* "You have come." *Shit. Shit. Okay.* Maybe she really just went crazy. Except when she looked over at Kai, he too looked shocked. *Great. Just fucking great.* A statue was talking to her. "Language, little Huntress, I am Anya, Guardian of the Danes." Anya's voice was like every ballad ever created, wrapped in her tiny vocal cords. The music swept over Rhia, and warmth flowed back into her soul. She breathed in deep. Everything shone and glowed. Her body. Her hair. Her eyes. Anya spoke life back into Rhia. "You are the first Huntress in over five thousand years. A great fate has been placed on your shoulders. You should have come when I first started calling you."

"Umm, yeah little lady, I only spoke to you today." Anya's brow arched up, high to her hairline.

"I have spoken to you many times, Huntress. To you and your Rahl. Do you not remember?" And Rhia felt the shock in Kai as he understood. That voice that rarely spoke to them since they had been bound. "Enough, I did not like your Rahl, but I have accepted him. I called you to warn you. You search for the bloodline of your enemy." Rhia's shoulders pulled back and she found herself kneeling before Anya respectfully. "Although Elias Santiago believed he was talking about the Blackstone's that is not the only blood that runs through your enemy's veins." Anya had their entire attention. This woman of magic, for Rhia didn't think radiation changed this being. Anya smirked as if she had read Rhia thoughts. "The blood of an out-clanned Dane flows in her. Caitlyn was your aunt. She defied your grandfather, Khale and married a man that did not sing to the fire in her heart. If the fire does not sing it burns the Dane from within killing them. No Dane has ever married or bonded without the rising fire. It is forbidden. Caitlyn married a Volvikov and birthed what I believed could be the destruction of all." The white eyes flared like lightening. "Rosadina. Pitch-black eyes and dark blood red hair. The minute she was born Dane's all around became weak. Wiping out the family due to a disease. The survivors were your father and grandfather. Ethan died of blood loss from a stabbing injury. And Khale... Khale passed away of old age. Althea... your grandmother."

The pause in between struck Rhia as a lie. She could feel the lie deep within her bones. This Althea was a part of her life. But Althea was not her grandmother. "She called every dark force that she could. She wanted Rosadina dead so that you could live. A true Dane must live. She believed she had succeeded until recently. Rosadina is the Empress and you are charged with her death." Anya's words were power. Floating over Rhia, reaching and pressing into her soul. "For the wrongs done, to protect your clan, your Rahl, you must no matter what take Rosadina's life." Taking a small dagger from her waist, Rhia slashed at her hand, mixing her blood with the water and stone of the fountain, and she swore. The oath of a Huntress.

"So, mote it be on the House of Dane, as the Sealgair Mor, I sayeth and bind it in blood. Rosadina Volvikov shall pass." The words tugged and flowed from her mouth. Binding their fates with no other path but death to walk upon, and the darkness of her sight slipped and pulled her to a peaceful sleep.

Who is BORCA?

Song Dedication: See You Again by Wiz Khalifa

Have you ever woken up knowing it was your last day? Certainly no one has. However, Genny was not no one. The minute she opened her eyes and realized she was in a hospital for whatever reason, she knew without a doubt that today she would die.

Rhia awoke inside the car with her headache nearly gone and the dim echo of the drums in her mind. It was over. She caught the scent of raspberry tea. Alek handed her a small canister from across her seat. Beside her, Kai was on the phone. She glanced over to see... hope. Maybe she ignored it or maybe she herself had lost it, which was why she had closed her eyes to the fact that they had given up hope even as they fought their battles in this war. He hung up and slid the phone into his third hidden pocket. Smiling over at her, he said, "*Madre* is awake. The doctors are checking up on her now." And the rocks crumbled from her, lifting the weight from her shoulders. *Madre* was going to be okay. Their family was still intact.

Caleb Maves Memorial Hospital
July 17, 3034

Madre was sitting up awake when they arrived. Rhia had

never been so relieved to see someone that she couldn't control the impulse to run up to and hug her. *Madre* grasped her in a tighter hold. "You are the Guardian of the Book of Blood." Her words were low so that only Rhia could hear her, and they sent a cold flush down Rhia's body. As Rhia pulled back and looked at *Madre,* shivers filled her heart. Something wasn't right, but how could she tell Kai that? He came up behind them and held *Madre's* hands in his own. They were tiny and fragile. Dark spots that Rhia had never seen stood out against her light skin. Her bright, golden-brown eyes were dull and lifeless. Could no one see this? *Madre* was not fine. Something was wrong.

Medic Narim stood on the other side, speaking to all of them. Rhia could barely hear him over the waves of her worry. *I mean, is he blind?*

"She doesn't seem to retain any memory of the incident. Other than that, she is healthy. I'm going to let her rest here for a few days and then I'll send her home on absolute bed rest." This wasn't a doctor! He hadn't a fucking clue what is going on. Rhia wanted to scream, but *Madre's* hands tightened around hers. *Madre* shook her head, no and the despair in her eyes told Rhia not to speak. It wasn't safe for any of them. Rhia swallowed her voice and tightened the chains of her vocal cords. And willed herself. And willed herself again. It was the only way to not scream. To not cry. To not rage, because something was wrong and Rhia was powerless. As Kai set a better protection detail, Rhia could not speak, and she began to understand sacrifice. Whatever should happen, it was a sacrifice that *Madre* and she were making for the good of the family. Rhia didn't yet know how this would affect her but she knew that it would. She knews that she would look back on this moment and she will always regret not voicing her concerns.

It was hell and heaven to stop Rhia. Her bright, strong-willed daughter-in-law saw what the medic and her children could not. Understandable, in a way. The medic was right. She was on the road to recovery. The poison had left her body, but Genny knew she wouldn't see the next morning. She'd done wrong and she had sinned in her own life. However, there wasn't a person in the world that could say Genny wouldn't do anything for her children. All of them. Her son Kai – that was the man his father had made him. Her Lucy. So gifted. So powerful. So lost. And Rhia. Rhia had not been hers for long, but Rhia had her heart. Rhia was a contradiction. So strong in many areas and weak in others. Not after that night. Genny could feel it in her bones. Her death would change many things. Rhia more than others. And that person. Genny knew someone else would cause her death. They may have thought Genny's death would break her children. How wrong they were. It would strengthen them like iron steel. Nothing would be able to touch them. So, for those reasons, she didn't fear her last moments. *How may it come to be?* Painful or soft. Light or dark. It did not matter, for she would welcome it. Genny welcomed her death and she smiled that she would be leaving without any regrets.

Blackstone Manor
7.10 PM

Rhia's stomach swirled and she fought back the bile. There was an awful taste in her mouth. Salt, pepper, and burnt meat. Since they walked in the house, everything had been off. Not just the fact that she didn't want to leave *Madre's* side. Someone had made blackberry tea. Normally it soothed her nerves and she usually had it after a workout. Today, however, the scent did not agree with her. Although she had thrown out the tea, the scent still permeated the air. And they were meeting Alexander and Francesco in an hour. And here she was sick. Her tongue became slick with saliva and her throat closed up but the bile rose and she wanted to vomit.

"Are you okay for tonight, because girl you look as if you're about toss up everything you ate, and I ain't seen you eat a damn thing," Priscilla's soft country voice sounded off from a far distance, which was odd because Priscilla was standing next to her.

"I'm fine." And yet her hands shook as they wiped the sweat from her face. It was truly too hot. "Open the window doors, will you, please?" she asked and she glanced at her jewelry to decide which would suit that night. The soft breeze of the night was welcome.

"You're not good, but I won't stop ya." Priscilla picked up a hair shell. Bright, sea sun-kissed blue. Two sharp points. A curved pink shell at the top with an amethyst attached to the far-left corner. Priscilla had parted Rhia's curls. The top was in a bun, held by the hair shell and the lower back was free. Priscilla had given her an old-world red dress. It reached just above her knees. A diamond spandex neck collar and a split on her right from her knee to her upper thigh. With red strap heels. Then with a ribbon at the back and a diamond holder. "Am I good or what?" Priscilla admired her work. As always, Priscilla gave her what Rhia needed and wanted.

"If you were not, I wouldn't have made you a part of the deal?" It had been such a short time. And yet it seemed so long since Rhia walked into Club Blue Lagoon and made her very first deal with Kai.

"Yes, you do beautiful work, Priscilla, but the art makes it worth it." Kai's smooth compliment left no question of who the art was in his eyes. He was wearing a Bennett Trializer for once. Black suit. Two metal plates at the collar flaps and another at his right pocket. "I have something for you." He opened a box with straps and ball pointed needles as thin as her hair shell sharp points. And her dagger, Mari, which she had hidden and never touched.

"What's this?" There was a hint of anger in her voice, but he ignored it and sat her down in her chair. Taking her leg and rolling up her dress just a couple inches, he took the wider strap and wrapped it around her leg.

"My gift, your protection." He added the longer needle to the strap. The ball pointed at the top. "I doubt that it will be possible for an attack, but it is better to be prepared. I noticed that you handle daggers and knives better than guns so I made this for you." The smallest strap he wrapped around her left wrist and added the smaller needles to them. "I know you never wanted to use this. Just as you told me that my dark power needs to be utilized, so does this dagger." Those ice blue eyes of his dragon shadowed his golden one. Staring at her and commanding her. For them, this was what was best. The last strap he bound around her arm and attached Mari to it. Rhia could feel Mari. Cold steel. But she would burn in the heat of the moment. When the battles called to her. "Er zai shi Rahl." In the command of the Rahl. He had been listening to Anya. She could still hear Anya fluttering in mind, trying to speak to her, but something had muffled Anya. Anya seemed to have no problem communicating with Kai.

"Where are we going?" The third strap against her arm was cloaked. If you were to look, you would only see her arm. The strap on her thigh was hidden by her dress. And to anyone else, the third one is an accessory. Smart of her man. Well-hidden, easily attained, perfectly protected.

"We are going to neutral ground. BORCA's laws are very strict and has the best technology to enforce those laws." Did she just hear him correctly?

"Who the hell is Borca to have such power?" Kai laughed softly as they walked toward the autodrive. Brennan, Sean, Alek, and Alessandra trailed on their sides. Kai helped her into the car. Sean sat across from them and Alessanda sat beside her. Alek and Brennan took the front seats and keyed in an address. The autodrive began to move but she was still waiting for Kai's answer.

"BORCA is not a person. It is a place. An old-world gaming hall."

BORCA's
2800 Western Frame
8.20 PM

The minute she entered BORCA, she could hear Trizha, but there was no radio. Curious, she looked around and stopped at a stand-still. On the stage was the real Trizha Bowers. "Francesco pulled some strings. Since I am the only one married and this is a men's conversation, he got some live entertainment for you." And he pushed her over to the pool table sitting. She was so shocked and grateful that she didn't get mad at the male, testosterone-filled attitude.

Undo our Love
Undo my heart

Undo my heart
Baby, please I ask you.
You've broken my heart over and over and over again.
The only thing I asked of you is to take away the pain.
Undo my heart
Undo my heart
Take away my memories
Take away the moments
I don't wanna know how you used to hug me.
I don't wanna know how you used to kiss me
I don't wanna know the feel of your touch.
I don't wanna remember anything involving you and me
So, I ask you to do this one thing for me.
Undo my heart
Undo my heart
I'm going to forget that your favorite color is blue like the sky
I'll forget that you love listening to music even when you're asleep at night.
Baby, please I ask you
You've broken my heart over and over and over again.
The only thing I ask of you is to take away the pain.
Undo my heart
Undo my heart
In the beginning when the snow first started falling
That was the day I believed you were for me
But now I know how this ends
I can't cry no more
Can't shed another tear
The ache in my heart won't be lifted.
And as I watch you walk away I know I can't be free.

So, I'm asking you to undo my heart
Undo my heart
Undo my heart
Rewind time to back when it all started
Back to when you first took my hand
Back to when without a thought, you breathe life into me.
Take me back to that day.
Baby please I ask you
You've broken my heart over and over and over again
The only thing I ask of you is to take away the pain
Undo my heart
Undo my heart
Take me back to that day
And don't you notice me
When you first see me again,
Turn the other way.
Finally, I'll never know the pain of our love
Then you will have…
Undone our love!

There were silent tears rolling down her eyes by the end of the song. "Do you need a napkin, Madam Blackstone?" She felt somewhat foolish for the tears and she turned to tell the person that. Light brown and dark black stripes hair swish around her. Hazel eyes. She was taller than Rhia by a foot. Big bouncy breasts. Smooth curves. And a smile as dazzling as diamonds. "Hello, little sister," Adriana said as she handed Rhia a drink.

Caleb Maves Memorial Hospital
7.50 PM

Genny heard the door creaking open. Her guards held it all nice-like for the fake nurse to enter. Blood red flaming hair. Black eyes. And a chilling smile. So this was what death looks like. The nurse closed the door and set the tray on the table next to Genny's bed, and she watched Genny as she readied the injection.

"You know why I am here, but not who I am?" Even her voices froze Genny. This was the true face of evil.

"Oh, I know you. You're my end. And you think this makes you the winner, but you'd be wrong. I won't fight you but know this. Blood is paid and when death comes for you it will not be like me. You'll die a thousand times in the seven gates of hell and still the fire will claim you. You will never be free or have another chance." She pushed the needle into Genny's skin, and waves of peace brought Genny under. Markus would be there, waiting in shadowlands when darkness claimed her so she had no further worries of this life.

"How sweet of you. The Heavenly Mother shall cry by your side as you see from the sky just how wrong you are." Those were the last words Genny heard in her second life. She could see Markus at the gates waiting for her. A warm smile and he pulled her in. Genny knew she was not wrong. Faith was on her side and the Heavenly Mother watched over her children. Protecting them from all harm. Even you – the Devil's mistress.

BORCA's
8.43 PM

Seeing Adriana, Rhia should have been excited, but she wasn't. Forgive her for being crazy, but this was worrisome. One – Adriana hadn't made contact with her since she spoke to Priscilla the previous month, and two – Kai said that this was a private meet, so the only people that should have been in there were them, their bodyguards, and the employees. How the hell had Adriana made it in? "Don't be so shocked. My hand reaches far. When word got sent to me that you would be here, I came to check up on you." Adriana's eyes skimmed across her dress and her pearl earrings. "You're looking good. Hubby must be treating you right. Do you still need saving?" Adriana handed her a teal mist, Rhia's favorite drink, and yet how did Adriana know that? Communication had been at bare minimum between the two since the separation at the bus. Rhia shook her head no. Even with the war and danger there wasn't another person in the world that she would rather be standing by. Kai had completed her life. Whatever may happen in this life, she wanted to face it with him every day. "Shocker, I thought out of all of us you'd be the one to stay single. And I especially didn't see you with another Blackstone." The top of Adriana's lips lifted in a smirk.

"Yeah..." Taking a sip from her teal mist, it burned down her throat, and that peaceful time away from the nausea turns spiralled back up. She pushed the teal mist away and clamped her hand over her mouth. Lord, what was wrong with her? Adriana's eyebrows creased in worry. Rhia waved her away. She took deep, clean breaths. That was the only thing helping. Black and yellow spots. She wavered and swayed. Holding tight to the table, Rhia shook her head, trying to clear it. Maybe she should have stayed home.

"Are you okay Bry?" There. That distant chugging sound of voice. Not just Priscilla, then. Trizha's voice floated with a high beat as another song began to play. "Bry… I think you need to sit down." And Adrianna moved to help lower her when POW. The shattering sound of glass and beating sounds of gunshots arrayed around. Adriana pushed Rhia to the floor and covered her body. Just one day she would have liked to the leave house and *not* be attacked.

Suspension, Covered Blinds, and Deadly Patience

Song Dedication: Crying by Ali

BORCA's
8.35 PM

Julian found the best distraction for Rhia for the meeting that night would change the next day. The war that had been simmering on the cliff's edge would be thrust upon morning rise. Tariq and Julian were waiting at the bar. Tariq was in a gray Bennett Trializer like Kai. His hair was down in full braids. The top was a thin band of braids while the lower one was in a French twist two sets of braids. Kai knew there was a story behind his hairstyle, as most of the time he only saw three tiny braids at his lower ends. Everyone had a reason for something, and he didn't judge Tariq for his. Julian was in a white Kandori suit. Julian's eyes never lied. The yellow-green eyes of his panther shone even in this semi dark room. Apparently, when the sifter in him awoke, he never was the same. He had a buzz of platinum white hair with black stripes near his edge. A platinum white and bright shining teeth that matched his pale white skin. "Evening, gentlemen." The bartender pushed an Alaskan vodka Kai's way. The frost was still floating as he tipped it back. "What have we found out?" Best to get business out of the way so that they could plan it out now.

"Your... cousin has a bit of reputation. Took some time to track her down even with a name." Julian's fingers circled his cup. Julian could get information on just about anything once he had a starting point. However, Julian's organization was not large enough for him to take on an opponent of this magnitude. Tariq had his hands on the best communications and weapon devices ever created, but he didn't have the territory to spread out his men for a frontal attack. In Kai's case, he got the territory and the men, but he was blindsided with no idea as to who was attacking them or why. This alliance was giving them the best advantages. "Dina Ignis. Dina the Fire Castor. Evil and deadly to the bone. Her own people fear for their lives." Taking out a folder, he pulled out pictures. Buildings and people.

"Which one is Dina?" Tariq asked as they searched among the pictures for their enemy.

"There isn't one. Ms. Dina Ignis is based in Washington but as of three months ago she came home to see her younger sister." *Sister? Rosadina has no siblings.*

Julian glanced over at him. The green hue of his eyes burned brighter and he pushed one last picture at him. It was a church with roughly twenty children and several adults standing in the front. Kai recognized three faces at once. The Jang brothers and Rhia. She hadn't changed much in the years. She was shorter with tiny waves of blue-black hair. Her hunter-green eyes dimmed in loss. There was no life in her eyes, but he could see the burning fire awakening in them. She couldn't be older than ten in this picture. What was the point of this? "Ms. Dina Ignis did not exist until eight years before that. So, I went another route tracking were Dina first appeared. Dina Ignis got a bus ticket with nearly fifteen other kids to Texas. The bus driver doesn't remember which one was Dina, but she remembers that bus ride.

All kids one direction and most important crying because their second big sister wouldn't join them. She described the sister as a green-eyed, fragile young girl. The strangest eyes she ever seen. Never seen green eyes like those, but in this world anything was possible." Rhia. Fuck, Julian was talking about Rhia.

"She's not a spy." It was instinct to defend his wife. Rhia was many things, but she didn't betray those that she had given her loyalty to. He knew without a doubt that he had hers.

"I didn't think she was, but Dina is the sister of her heart. She's going to come for Rhia if she hasn't already. When she does, Rhia is will have to choose. The question is whom? The sister she grew up with or the man that forced her into a marriage." He glared at Julian. Yeah, Kai heard where Julian was coming from, but Julian didn't know jack shit about them. There was so much to them. Especially after they met Anya…

His heart clenched in pain as he remembered the oath that Rhia made to Anya. *So, mote it be on the House of Dane, as the Sealgair Mor, I sayeth and bind it in blood. Rosadina Volvikov shall pass.* He almost shattered his glass with the realization. Shit. He stood. He had to find Rhia. *There must be a way around that oath.* Was it really only this morning that she had said those words only for them to backfire on them? "Don't worry. I mean the attacks were not just against you. Didn't Dina send a dark beast after Rhia?" His insides twisted with worry. At the time it had really seemed as if the dark beast was there for that very reason, yet would Dina kill her own sister? Yes, apparently. To weaken him. Maybe not now. His power. Why didn't he think about how it would look on the outside?

"Heavenly Lord, we are in trouble." His voice was hoarse as his was hit one after another with realizations. "That's why she took a break. Not to regroup. She wants to get close. And Rhia…

dammit." He banged his hand against the bar table in frustration.

"Care to fill us in?" Julian stepped closer to their circle, blocking off as much sound as possible.

"Rhia… is a… huntress." They stared at him in confusion. Not enough time for that story. "Later. Anyway, she has been tasked with Rosadina's death. No way out of it." Tariq's eyes widened in shock. He had family. An uncle, who passed away, and a nephew, so he understood the bonds of family. If you truly loved and cared for family, it would hurt. Even if it was your own hand that took that life, it would hurt, and he never wanted that for Rhia. Julian had no one. Kai heard that Julian killed his own father in vengeance. So, the blank look in his eyes allowed Kai to understand him a little bit more. "Dina isn't going wait for that. She's been watching us and Rhia has ruined her plans going back to my assassination attempt. By now she must think Rhia is too powerful of enemy. She's going to come for Rhia… as a friend… and that is when she will attack."

"Won't that put your wife in a spot? She won't think her sister is her enemy?" And that would make Rhia the perfect tool in Dina's eyes. That meant that to save them, Kai may have had to betray Rhia. Until she could see the truth.

"When would be the best time to get close?" Tariq asked. *True – Rhia doesn't leave the Manor as much as Kai does. Lately she only goes to two places. The hospital and the church for Sunday Mass. So, the only chance is…*

"During an attack." His hand tingled and he reached for his azai `22. Just then he could hear a buzz. Tariq pulled out a black communication device, shaped in an octagon, that could easily be held in the hand. He flipped it open and a projection of a woman appeared. The project glitched and her picture wasn't entirely clear. She was not near any communication lines, but judging by Tariq's brightening eyes, he recognized her.

"Nizhoni." The words were a soft whisper on Tariq's lips. Shock and pleasure.

"It's a trap. Tariq, run it's a trap." With those words she faded out and bullets shatter through the windows. Like a well-organized team that had worked together for a thousand years, they took cover and pull out their weapons. Julian was carrying two Colt 45 Revolvers and Tariq pulled out a sword. Longest damn sword Kai had ever seen, and he didn't know how Tariq was hiding it on his person. Kai pulled out his Azai 22. Julian held four fingers. Four guys inside. Good thing he left all the guards with Rhia. One... two... three... four and go. Tariq slashed his swords across the chest of the man nearest him. Not one blood splatter. Kai shot the one by the door and the other crouching by a table. Julian took out the last. It was quick and way too easy in his book.

"Well looks like you were right. Dina must be somewhere in here with your wife." *Aw, fuck.* Kai's feet moved before the thought even processed in his mind. He had to get to Rhia.

BORCA's
9.08 PM

Mari was burning like a falling meteorite against Rhia's arm. There were more than a dozen men. For some reason it was just her and Adriana. Her guards. Even Kai's guards were down before anything even went down. Again, in a three-month span, Rhia bent down, hiding behind a small, round table. Alek and Sean, the only two to somehow manage to keep up, were just behind shooting in a spiral of epic fire. Mari was whispering to her. Mari wanted to be used. To protect her. Rhia knew it was too soon to use Mari, so she went for the thick needles that Kai had hidden on her body. She closed her eyes, gathered her breath, and then she *saw*. True Sight had more advantages than she once believed. In the darkness against the back of the enemy line, it made the perfect tool to find targets. All she had to do was wait for their moves. It was so simple. An inch of their body and she flicked off her finger. They came in with bullets, not capsules or anything. They wanted her alive. As the needles slowly diminished from around her, Anya gathered the knowledge that she needed. Anya's essence tied to hers, and Kai wavered over the people, pulling information right from their minds like the strings of a child's toy.

Now... the demand of Mari. Before Rhia knew what she was doing, she had pulled Mari from the wrap, twisted and stabbed the man that was shadowing just behind her in the heart. Mari soaked in his essence. Pulling his breath, his memories, his life into her own. Eating at the darkest moments and with a wailing screech rebounding it onto their enemies. They fell under Mari's scream, pressed to the floor, unable to rise. Kai crashed through the door with his guns high and aiming.

"We're good!" she shouted before he hurt someone. He literally stomped over to her. Helping her to stand, he checked her over. "See? Fine." At her side, Alek was helping Adriana and Alessandra to stand. Sean and some men she didn't recognize collected their enemies from the floor, binding them in chains. Adriana grunted in pain. As Rhia checked Adriana over, she could see that Adriana had been shot. "We need a medic, Kai. Adriana is hurt."

"Who?" The warm, gruff voice she has gotten use to was laced with cold ice now. Right, Kai didn't know Adriana.

Spinning around, Rhia helped Alek to keep Adriana standing before Kai even though she was bleeding. Kai was the Blackstone *Don* and his word was law. Although she commanded their people, the final words were still his as long he stood.

"Kai, meet Adriana. My sister." And for the first since the bond opened to them, Kai shut her out, and she was lost to what exactly was going on with him.

9.27 PM

"Kai, meet Adriana. My sister." When those words left her lips, Kai wanted to kill this woman right there and then, but he couldn't. Rhia would never forgive him and this... Adriana had to know that she had his hands tied. Julian brushed by him standing at his side. Just to his other side behind Rhia and Adriana, Tariq shook his head no. They heard. They knew. And like him they understood the time was not now. Patience. They must have patience to succeed. For them to win this war and survive they would pretend to be ignorant. So, he gritted his teeth and memorized her. Bright brown and black streaks of hair. Golden-brown eyes. Chocolate skin. This didn't fit the description that Anya had given, but he knew without a shadow of doubt that Adriana, Rhia's sister, was Dina – their enemy.

"Yes, we can fix her up at home." And still facing Rhia, he closed off the bond. Anya had taught him, but Anya didn't think they would ever need to use it. Anya had described it as a small pain for a Kias and Rahl to close off the bond between them. It wasn't a small pain. It was fire licking at the edges of his soul.

9.59 PM
Blackstone Manor

Allowing that woman into their domain was like pulling the nails from his fingertips. Extremely painful, but he would live. Brennan and Sean escorted Adriana to be cleaned up. He couldn't breathe. He never knew rage could take your breath away. Lucy came running from the living room tears flowing big and wide from her eyes. She wrapped her arms around him and hiccupped high near his ears.

"Luce, what's wrong?" He rubbed against her back to get her to calm down. Rhia had frozen next to him, her eyes haunted as if she knew what was wrong.

"*Madre's... Madre's* dead, Kai. She's dead." And her sorrowful wails reached the heaven's. Something broke in Kai. Gone. His *Madre* was gone. Rhia swayed and crashed in Alek's arms.

Those words floated around the Manor. The light of this house. Holding tight to Lucy all the blood that had coated his hands, he bound his own oath to Rhia's.

As the anchor of the huntress, I adorn my weapons and shall aide in the ending of Rosadina Volvikov, and his eyes focused and glared at the door that Adriana had gone behind.

Yes, no matter what he had to do. He would find a way to kill you, Dina Ignis.

Jealous Rage

Song Dedication: I'll be Waiting by Arjun, and I Can't Forget You by Arjun ft. Jonita Gandhi

Part 1: Jealousy
July 29, 3034
Brackenmoor Cemetery
10.19 AM

It was the quietest funeral Rhia had ever been to, and this was her third. No one cried. No one said a word in *Madre's* honor. As her casket was laid in the ground, every man and woman of the Blackstone Organization was fueled with hate. There were many that they had buried. Their comrades. Their friends. Their boss Markus. Each person had been active in protecting the Family and the people. *Madre* wasn't. She heard the screams and cries of the damned. She helped some of these mothers send off their husbands and sons. She was *innocent*. And the Royals... Rosadina... their enemy had walked into their home... into her hospital room... and they snuffed the life from her eyes. Rhia grieved the most, for she knew the truth. *Madre* died willingly. She had sacrificed herself for *them*. It was hell all over again to not say anything to Kai. Not that it would matter. In the weeks' time since they had received the news, Kai had not spoken to her. Locked in his office. Far away from her. Emotionally and physically.

As the white roses were thrown in with *Madre,* Rhia whispered her final words to her. "I can't forgive myself even if it was for the family, *Madre.* I never knew my mother but I accepted you as mine. And that is why whomever Rosadina is, wherever she is I will honor my oath and let you meet her in the between." She layed a kiss on her white rose and tossed it in with her promise. She had cried herself tired this week to the point that she had no more tears. That was fine. She would cry again when Rosadina was dead. And turning her back, Kai and Rhia, helped Lucy walk toward the car, her soft cries the only sound between them. They trudged and lifted to keep Lucy standing. As the door shut, Rhia knew this was only the first step. Raindrops may fall, but there was a timing. For them this death was the last stake. Now they wouldn't just end the Royals. They would destroy them.

11.00 AM
Blackstone Manor

Once Kai had Lucy down to rest, he went upstairs to change into his exercising material. Rhia wasn't there. Since the news crashed on them, she had been with Lucy or in her room, nowhere else, and Kai had just gotten Lucy to sleep... so where was she? The only peace he received these days were the small glimpses that he caught of her. He was the one that cut off the communications between their bond and the price was a rising flame. Burning from the inside. He didn't have many more days of resistance left in him. If he couldn't make Rhia see the truth soon then the bond would drive him crazy, and where would they be?

Gym, 1st Floor

"Don't let anyone in. I need to clear my head." Sean nodded at him as he entered the gym. He was wrapping his fighting gloves around his fingers when he heard it. The scream of frustration. The pounding of a fist slicked with hate and despair. He glanced up. He heard that after some years together, couples become in sync. Moving perfectly together. Not needing to speak or think before they reacted. He thought for Rhia and him if there was such a road it was a long one away. He was wrong. Rhia in striking perfect and quick as the wind was jabbing and kicking the bag. No tears, but a soothing pain to the point. Quick. Fast. A flurry of motion. He couldn't see where she would hit as she twists, jumped, turned, and flew. This is what made her name. Red Wing. Bloodied and battered, but still she rises. High and proud like the God of War, Ares. Calm and cold, steady amid a raging sea storm. Soaring against the dark thunderous sky. Red Wing defied all in her purpose for she always survives.

Mesmerized by her beauty and intensity, Kai couldn't stop himself from getting a better look. Closer and closer he moved until he was nearly at her back. Her arm swung and he stepped back to avoid, but he underestimated the distance. Like three bound steel, the hit sent him to the floor. Blood swarmed his mouth. He swallowed. No need to make her realize the strength she could obtain. Shaking the spots from his head, he found Rhia crouched over him. "Shall we dance?" The words slipped from him. For days he had held the silence in. Eating at him. Separating them. Turning away from him, she picked up short swords. The handles turned inward so that the blades brushed just inches from the skin's edges. Amateurs were not meant to weld them. Rhia was no amateur. Her stance faced him with burning determination.

"Shall we?" She whispered. He moved to the outer area and picked up a shrapnel staff. A wide triangle knife at each end. He spun it to get a firm grip and faced Rhia. His heart. His weakness. His strength. And they both attacked. A spiral of spins and stabs. A cut here or there. The rage. The pain. The despair. Even the defeat. All that they could not say. With each attack they shouted to each other, to the heavens, to those damned Royals. So intent on making someone else feel exactly what they felt.

ENOUGH.

The voice shattered his concentration and bounced off circles in his mind. Bells rang around his ears. Rhia staggered and barely sustains standing.

The both of you, leave this room and find somewhere to meditate. Before you kill each other. Anya coated her words with a gentle request, but they both knew it for the command that it was. He found himself in his room tethering on the brink of loss.

This cannot go on. You must tell her the truth, Rahl Malachi. He knew what she was asking of him, but he could not. At the moment, if Rhia knew the whole act, it would dismantle her and them like no other thing had. Like no other death could.

Not yet. Dina will make a move. Something that could pull Rhia from her. I have to believe that. It is the only way to end this mess. There was no other way around it. He knew that betrayal was the only answer to opening Rhia's eyes. And she was the key to Dina's end. His instincts screamed that to him as a reminder every morning. And he could only wait.

At what price, Rahl Malachi, at what price? Anya asked, and it lay heavy upon his heart. Yes, there would be a price and even he could not know just how high it was. He heard his door creaking open and hands wrap around his waist. The warmth feels the same as her. Yet...

"I'm sorry for your loss." That voice didn't belong to Rhia. Unlocking the arms from around his waist, he turned until he could see her. Her eyes were first, and he knew it was not Rhia. Golden-brown. Not a speck of green in sight. "However, I can make you feel better?" She didn't have to reach far before her lips capture his. He had to force back the gag. For all purposes, this woman was his blood related cousin. He was not supposed to know that, though. And this was his one and last chance. So, he allowed himself to kiss her, to make her believe he had fallen, and he opened the floodgates of the bond between Rhia and him. So that Rhia could see. So that Rhia could know.

He was much too easy. A beautiful face, a warm disgusting heart, and an alluring kiss reels him right in. It wouldn't be long until she had him so wrapped around her fingers that he would push Rhia right out of his life and straight into her arms. He was a good kisser, though. As his lips brushed softly against hers, the only thing wrong was that he was a man. This would be more pleasurable in the arms of a woman. Like Maya. She was so delightful. So young. Just as easy to seduce as her darling male cousin. As Dina slipped her tongue into his mouth and untied his shorts, she heard a loud bang in the distance echo. Kai jumped back from her in surprise. *What the hell?* "Rhia..." The name was a bare whisper on his lips. And she turned toward the door. Rhia stood there in a silk, knee-length bathrobe. And Rhia was furious.

When the emotions first started pouring, Rhia was not sure she was feeling what she believed. Excitement. Full and bursting. She paused while drying my hair. Maybe she was imagining things. Then the flashes collided. Kai with another woman, kissing her. Her chest twisted in an ache so painful she had to gasp for air. *No, it's not true.* She threw on her silk robe. Her feet slapped against the floor and she pushed Alek out of her way. He collided into the wall across from the room. She didn't care. She was blinded to all, but the flashes coming by the second were in her mind.

Trust in your Rahl, Huntress Rhia.

Hmph! That is a joke. The emotions. The flashes. And now Anya. Goddess, take her! She froze before his office door. Did she open it or not? In her head, Rhia saw the woman's hands reaching where it should not have. *She's a dead woman!* And with a roundhouse kick, Rhia slammed the door open. The door bounced back and then opened again. Rhia would recognize that woman anywhere. The air left her. A hammer punched at her chest. Dark brown and light black spots appear before her eyes. And then she blacked out. She could feel herself moving. Like air. Like wind. Like a storm. "Rhia, no!" Kai screamed and something bound her hands, twisting them around and pulling them back, pushing her down to her knees. The scratch of scales. The ice-cold burn of frost.

Not today, little huntress. The quavering voice of his dragon reached her beyond the darkness. As her eyes cleared she saw them, Kai by his desk and Adriana near the couch.

"Get out! If you value your life, you will leave and never look back." With a blazing fury, Rhia screamed at Adriana. At first, as if Adriana did not hear Rhia, she stared at her. When Adriana's eyes glanced over at Kai, they were filled with shock. So out of control, Rhia didn't look at Kai. She watched Adriana as she watched him, and a quivering thirsting power moved from Rhia arm down to her fingertips. "Leave, now!" Fire burst from her fingers. Gliding down the floor, not burning anything, and it reached the tips of Adriana feet. Adriana jumped back as it burned her. Then she ran. Her feet pounded against the floor as she zigzagged down the stairs. Rhia pulled and gripped the fire back into her hands. How to extinguish it? His dragon breathed ice, blowing out the fires. Then flew back to his master. Hovering in a protective manner.

Trust, Anya asked her. She couldn't feel any more trust with this man, but she was bound to him. Therefore, she could not leave him. With her head high, she stood and left. He had beaten her soul, but he had not broken her.

Part 2: Rage
August 2, 3034

Was it only just a few days ago? It didn't feel so. As the morning light broke through their balcony floor and into her eyes, Rhia woke up empty. She was a shell sleeping in this house. She locked herself in her room and kicked that cheating bastard out. How some forgave them was beyond her capabilities. Alessandra would bring her breakfast and dinner. She'd let Rhia know when he was out so that she could check up on Lucy. With all the ruckus going on, she would think that Lucy was better off outside this house. But no, Rhia feared what would happen if they sent Lucy away.

Bam, Bam, Bam

The sound of the drums became louder after Kai's betrayal. She didn't know what their meaning was now. At first, she believed them sounding off meant that that were closer to their enemy. She had the pounding drill of a hammered migraine again. Alessandra and Alex thought she was in bed because of him. In truth she just couldn't get up. Everything was so loud and bright.

"May Lin, close the balcony doors and pull the dark blinds down." She was parched. Her mouth was dry as a desert and yet she was able to just get those words out.

"Yes, *Dona*." Maybe it was her ears but May Lin was sounding more human than computerized lately. She closed her eyes in the peaceful darkness and return to sleep. So quiet. So nice. Let her rest. For a short period.

Blep... Blep... Whosh...

She awoke again to such odd sounds. "Med, you're not hearing me. Something is wrong with my *Dona* and it is not because she is simply tired. Run some damn test or I will call the *Don* of Blackstone and you can answer to him." A tiny rough voice. That quiet man was actually speaking.

"Alek..." A cough built up and she couldn't hold it back. The hackle grated against her body and put the medic on edge.

"You may be right. I will get a nurse in here immediately." With the swish of his coat, he was gone.

"I told you that from the damn beginning. Dumbass medic." There was heat and anger in his words. His shadowy finger moved in her sight, but she couldn't really see him. Not even his aura. What was wrong with her? "I went to check up on you around noon. You were asleep and burning to a point that you were sweating through your clothes. Alyssa and I rushed you to the hospital. No worries the boss doesn't know yet." The man didn't talk much but he was able to read a situation quick and nicely. That was why she chose him. He had that sense around him.

"Thank you, you're a good bodyguard." Alek's eyes flashed over her. Yes, she had gained a very loyal and good bodyguard, but also a very good friend. Hours later, the medic finally handed her some unexpected news.

"I have good news and bad news. Your decision on which you want first." *Got to say, I agree with Alek.* This was one dumbass medic and she didn't like him. Behind her seat, standing over her protectively, Alek scoffed at the medic's behavior. She had no time for a disagreement. If she didn't get home soon, then she would end up explaining to Kai where she had been all day. That was not a discussion she wished to make.

"Go ahead with the bad news." And she braced herself.

"You have anemia. That won't be any good to your present condition." *Excuse me? Anemia? That is the bad news?* Okay, someone, anyone, hand her a nice silver steel bat. She was taking it to his head. "Pregnancy in the early months are very delicate. We could have handled your anemia better if not for the baby. Instead, I'll send you over to a family medic who can prescribe something for you…"

"Did you just say… ba… baby?" She almost wasn't able to choke the words out.

"Your blood test results came back positive for pregnancy." He wrote something on a note and hands it to her. She had checked out. Blank. Nothing there. Frozen in time. Alek handled the rest, listening to the medic's orders and helping her out of there. She didn't say, hear, or see anything during their return home. Even when she went to lay down, she was still in that medic's office hearing those words. Pregnant. Baby. They were having a baby. Suddenly she jumped up in a panic. Alek entered her room with some soup by the smell of it.

"You have to eat *Dona*. For the little one," he said as he brought the tray over. That was right. There was a life growing inside her. As she picked up her spoon, the panic grew until she was shaking before Alek. "What is it? What's wrong?" Tears poured out of her eyes she tugged on his sleeve.

"Don't tell Kai. Please!" Who knew what he would do once he found out. No. For this child, it was time to go. It was time to run.

6.23 PM

Rhia was walking on egg shells, each step shaky and fearful. She thought that at any second Kai would burst through the door and scream at her about the baby. Thankfully she made it back before him, but that put her on more edge. There was only one person she knew that could make her truly disappear cleanly. Her sharp fingernails bit into the skin of her hands as she contemplated how she would contact Adriana. Her thoughts in a cloud, she didn't hear him come in.

"Luce said you went to see an immediate medic." His low, raspy voice floated to her ears. It took her breath away. Just a few days and yet it felt like years had passed. His personal scent floated under her nose and she relaxed. The tension slipped from her, and her eyes fluttered open in delight. He was dressed in old world clothes. Tight, black, short-sleeve shirt and loose, black slacks. There was her sexy man. The smile fell from her face. He was not her man. In a way, maybe he never was. From that first moment they met, he changed everything. For her child, she couldn't stay.

"Just a slight fever and anemia." She pushed on the emotional distance between them. The echo of an ache beat against her heart and she knew that it belonged to him. She wouldn't allow herself to be pulled under. She had more responsibilities now.

"Ahh… get dressed. We have an event tonight." And he walked away, going to the room next door that he had taken over.

7.47 PM

Priscilla had her seated with her back faced away from the mirror. Priscilla's design today was different. Although she couldn't see it, she could feel it. Soft and elegant.

"When I'm done, Kai won't know what hit him." Her back stiffened and straightened up at Priscilla's words.

"I don't wish to impress him." She growled and the lipstick grazed past her lips.

"Be still." Priscilla took a towel and dipped it into the water bowl and dabbed around the edges of her lips. "This thing… between you and Kai… y'all need to settle it." Her eyes burned with a haunting glare, softly whispering to her as the brush moves over her face. "There's something not right with this picture. You said yourself if he hadn't opened the bond then you never would've known. Any man that cheats wants to keep it a secret." The careful cool touch of jewels beneath her eyes and by her temples. "The puzzles aren't coming together right. There's more to this. Stand." Still Priscilla didn't let her face the mirror. Priscilla helped her into her dress. Soft. Warm. Silk. *Ching. Ching.* The sound of swishing layered beads. Priscilla's hands glided and pushed her back into her seat. Then they fluttered in her hair. She closed the world off. Just Priscilla's hands. Priscilla's voice and Rhia.

"If you take a chance and look, maybe just maybe, you'll find the truth behind the close doors." As Priscilla hummed above her and worked her hair to perfection, she had to constantly shut down Priscilla's words. She would love nothing more than for there to be a hidden truth for the days that had passed. She no longer had that choice. There wasn't a reason in the world that would make her change her mind and stay with Kai. Her heart was already aching with the pain of separation. She had to do what was best for her child and that was getting them out of this house and away from this family. "Do you tonight. Do it in classic beauty." And spinning her around, her heart fluttered with happiness. Light blue, tight bust, curved high shoulder straps. White gold circle strings beads at the knee. With a swish of daring, her dress had a white silk sash reaches the floor. She was the picture of a 1920s ball queen. Curls bundled and sophistically thrown over her left shoulder. An emerald pendant swaying just above her breast. And the bright glow of her skin threw her for a giggle.

"Wow!" The whisper breathes upon her lips and floats up to the ceiling in quiet moment. This was just a WOW moment.

Blue Lagoon
8.45 PM

"*Je ta mi*, hummingbird." Smooth light brown hair. Dark, dark, coal black eyes. Flat and small against his brown skin. Six feet of muscles and powerful strength. Wide, blindingly bright teeth.

"Roland." Roland was a name of beauty and power. His name once clashed with his looks. Tall and lanky. Squandered, but broad shoulders. Growing up knowing what would happen when they turned thirteen, no one wanted to pick on the tallest kid there. In fact, they wanted his protection, because they could tell he was one of the few that would stay. Oddly enough, that pushed him from others. Except for her. She didn't want his protection. She wanted a teacher. And Roland wasn't just the best fighter, he was the exact same age as her. They were born the same day and same year. So, he was her best timeframe. She went to him with no lies. And he agreed. In a way, he created Red Wing. "*Je ta mi*, scorpion." Unlike the others, Roland visited her once a year. He was her contact. Everyone got to see him even if they cut off contact with others.

"Adriana wanted me to check on you. Said you had a disagreement." He scoffed under his breath.

"I'm not so good, scorpion." He froze under her sorrowful tone, and this time he really looked at her.

"What she'd do?" Frost layered his words.

"Take the blinds off so that I had a good view of her." His hands shook and a black thing shimmered around his fingertips. He couldn't explode here. "Forget all of that. I need a favor." His knuckles tightened and darkened. His eyes burned with bright, black intensity.

"What?" His voice was deadly calm, though.

"An out. I need to leave Louisiana." Shock fazed his impression. Everyone but her had wanted to leave. To run. Even Roland had wanted to walk away. She had stood against her wounds and scars. She had always fought. She was a survivor. Nothing and no one could get her down. Now, though, the fight was gone. Vanquished before the eyes of motherhood. Fear that her child would be unwanted. Determination to never allow her child to know what that felt like.

"You making this the final contact." Final contact, which was if they got her out and she cut off all connections to them.

No acknowledgement even if she ran into Roland seven years from now.

"I haven't a choice. There's... something I must protect. And it'll do you guys no good with me holding you back." He stopped a waiter with a tray full of drinks, grabbed a glass of wine, and then looks at her in silent question.

"Orange juice, please." He handed her the juice.

"I'll make it happen." As she took a sip, Kai made his way to them in furious bound steps.

"Go." She whispered the command to Roland. He stepped back into the shadows, soaking in the darkness and becoming one with the background wall.

"We're leaving." And he dragged her away with a binding grip. He practically tossed her into the autodrive. It rose like an exploding volcano after being kept at bay for so long, the nausea swarming in her throat. That is the one thing she would be happy to let go. Covering her mouth silently with shaky hands, she sat there waiting for the moment they would make it to the manor. As she closed her eyes, she wondered if *Madre* was alive – would she be excited about the baby, or like Rhia worry about a child growing up in this lifestyle? Would *Madre* ask her to hide or to stand by Kai and fight with him? *Fight, mi nonna*. Almost in a dream, *Madre's* voice began to whisper around her. Calling and pleading. *For the famiglia.*

She awakened to someone fiercely pulling her from the autodrive. Kai pulled her inside the manor and then surprising her, took her bridal-style, he continued to carry her to the third floor. Never letting her go.

"Put me down or by the Mother I will..." She was screaming as he kicked open his office door. He slammed her on the couch. Jostling her nerves. His hand wrapped around her neck lightly.

"What the hell Kai?" With a blazing glare she faced him. Rage clouded them both, igniting the emotions they had kept within.

"Is this revenge, huh? Disrespecting me in front of our men, our partners. People under my damn protection. Is this how you wish to get back at me?" Kai hollered at her. His teeth bit at every word. His eyes darkened to night black with his fury.

"So, the fuck what? So, what if I disrespect you? You have no rights over me. Absolutely none. Not my mind. Not my soul. Definitely not my body." She huffed with a feeling of wrongness. *How dare he?* Had he forgotten what he had done to her? "If I wanted to fuck a man before the entire city you have no right to deny me." Before she knew what had happened, Kai had lifted her and slammed her into the wall. It dented and dust broke away, her feet dangling from the floor.

"Not ever. I'd kill him. Skin him to his bones. Burn him to ash and scatter it over the seven territories. He would never be whole again." Anger. Fury. Pain. Guilt. It pounded against their bond. Flowing against the tide from one overturned sea to another.

"I hate you." Clear as rain drops, these words reached Kai's ears. Her eyes belayed her lie. Her cool, dark black eyes flicker steadily in, matching his own and foretelling the truth that she wished to hide. It softened his rough manner and casted his anger away. Gently he grazed his fingers, curving under her chin and lifting her face till she was the center of his attention.

"No, you don't. You only wish you did." As her tears fell in surrender, he wiped them away with his fingers. "Just as you, I wish I could tell you everything on my mind. Everything that's happening, but I can't. You're not ready." Softly retracing their steps back to the beginning, gaining her trust over again. He put all of that into the kiss. Warming the coldness that was about to shatter their hearts and souls. His hands slipped under her dress. Ripping away the soft silk of her panties. Dipping his tongue farther down her throat. Quickly, he unsnapped his belt and let his pants hit the floor. He filled her. Her heat was hot to the touch. She wrapped her legs tighter around his waist. The end of her heels dug into his back. Slowly he dragged the pace out. Holding them both, he gripped her waist and pushed and pushed and pushed until they quaked with shivers. Until the breath left them. He wouldn't give in. He wouldn't hit just right purposely. Tension strung them together and tears trailed against her cheek in the darkness. Not yet. Hot. Wet. Her juices coat his cock. Slick and smooth he moved. Her muscles tightened as she used her heels to try to press him closer. Not yet… he made the pace slower. The edge was just around the corner but he denied them.

"I'm sorry. I won't do it again. I swear. Just let me…" she promised in a whisper, and he quickened his pace. Hitting directly in her spot. Within a minute, Rhia found her fulfillment. This didn't put the puzzle pieces back together, but made them face the splintered cracks.

Breathing heavily against the wall, he told her, "It's not safe just yet. When this is over and soon it will be I won't hide anything. I won't." With the promise ringing in the silent air, he carried his wife to their room. When all of this was over this was where their new beginning would start. And he swore that no other man or woman would break them again. No matter the reason.

Ambush

Song Dedication: No Good by Erik Right

Blackstone Manor
8.19 AM

It was the coldest day Rhia had ever woken to since the news of *Madre's* death. The wind crept through the cracked windows. With the sheets wrapped around her body, she lay on the bed, contemplating the night before. What did Kai mean? Did she still have covered blinds on when it came to Adriana? She found a black, V-neck shirt and blue jeans along with black boots that reach just under the knees. The interesting part was Mari. Wrapped in white and barely tinged red, her soul dagger was striking against the white cotton sheet. So was the Azai 22 next to it. Guns were not her weapon of choice, yet still Kai gave her one. Why? There was a note on the bed.

Alexander and Francesco. 4.00 p.m. Meet tonight.

Kai had coded it for her. He was meeting with Tariq and Julian at nine a.m. today. The elegant twist of the words waved and blurred before her eyes. And the gray field filled her mind. She saw Kai in the distance. Alek was laying on the ground before him, bloodied and bruised; he was desperately trying to tell Kai something. She couldn't make out the words. Kai's eyes brightened with blinding intense fury. As her sight began to come back in color, she wished for more. To see more. To know more.

The small glimpse that she was able to get was not enough. What did she really need to see out of that vision? She missed it that day. Afterwards, she learned to pay attention to every detail. Every second. Down to the last count. A true seer saw what she could change. She didn't see the despair in his eyes. Nor past the fury and into the will of a man who would die for his family. She didn't see it. So, she wasn't careful. And it cost them all. Cost them more than those disarming months did. The cost broke them. Remade them. A Phoenix was awakened. She didn't see herself dallying on what she could not understand, so that day she went to the kitchen. To prepare for their guest.

"I thought I'd help you cook. Something *Madre* did, right?" Lucy stood in the kitchen doorway asking her. You could tell she had been in her room quite a bit. The reason didn't matter. Lucy was out and actually wished to do something.

"We have a feast to make. *Madre*…" That sorrow-filled pain burned her throat. "We cooked for the entire household. Family, guards, and guest. Today Julian and Tariq are coming over with a few of their men." Nodding her head, she went to the refrigerator, pulling out fruits, vegetables, bacon, eggs, and bread. She didn't get any sausage this time. Prices had gone from thirty-five dollars to over fifty dollars. She knew it was rare and they had the money, but she was still somewhat conscious of her past when dealing with small money. She set her maximum allowed amount to spend and steadfastly refused to go over. Though it was quiet as the two of them worked, it was a soothing quietness. Patient and tender. It almost made her hum a tune like she did whenever it was her and *Madre* cooking. She didn't have a complete heart to bring it up. So, they cooked and placed it on the ceramic center counter-top table. Filling it until it was nearly bursting. Once they had finished, she took some coffee to Kai in his office. It was almost time for his meeting. It was an innocent moment. They didn't speak. Nor did they look at one another. Last night she became almost willing to stay. Willing to give them a chance. So, to her it was okay. To leave that innocent moment as it was. If only...

"She wants out of this place. And a cut off. From us. What did you do?" Scorpion didn't scream. Nor did he yell. However, the people in the room were hit with his cold brush aura similar to the Empress.

"I wanted her back with us. My plan backfired is all." Dina walked away from his anger.

"Backfired! You fucking blew it, Rosa. Rhia's running and in all the years I have known her, Rhia has never run from anything or anyone. So again, tell me what you did?" He was standing over her desk. The quick flick of black mist formed around his hands. The wood decayed under the imprints. Her bottomless evil, black eyes glanced upon him.

"I seduced Malachi Blackstone." At first, he thought he misheard her. When he realized that he didn't laughter bubbled out from within him.

"Why are you laughing?" Staring at her it was a pity that she seriously didn't know.

"Malachi dragged Rhia back home for speaking to me. If you think you seduced him, you're the only one." And pushing back into the group, he smirked down at her. "You got played, Dina." With those words he stepped outside her office. The shattering of glass echoed her fury.

Blackstone Manor
9.08 AM

Tariq came in with ruffled feathers and a bold glare upon his face. "I need a drink. Got any?" His feet circled as he stomped in a pacing manner.

"Only burnt ice." The man was wired, and Kai would do anything to keep him from exploding in his home. He had barely sat the drink down before Tariq snatched it up and consumed it. Slamming the glass onto his desk. "Something on your mind?" Kai took a sip of the coffee that Rhia had brought him. Black with a drop of milk and no sugar.

"Private things." The digital shimmer of a female flashed through Kai's memories as he recalled the messenger that had warned them. That breathless whisper of endearment that escaped Tariq as she appeared on his communication device. The tightly-bound longing and worry that had crossed his face in quick, jittery seconds. Tariq had a woman. All his informants had guessed that he had no involvement for pleasurable purposes. Maybe he was better able to hide her. They had an alliance. Their ties may not break after they ended the war soon. A friendship would keep away the storming waters when they came.

"Maybe I can help? Talk." Tariq shook his head and asked for another drink. As Kai passed it over to him, Julian walked in through the door.

"You may as well. Business can't continue with power suffocating the room." His hands moved like blowing away smoke. The pressure rose with his delegation.

"Close the door. People don't need to know this." It would be an insult to his protection, but it wasn't his people that had Tariq cautious. No, their people were trustworthy. However, even he could slip up with the Manor's protection detail, and a one-way listening device could get in. Still a few rooms had been set up to prevent this. His office was number one on the list and both were aware of this. Julian came in and shuts the door. "Three years ago, I went to Alexandria to track down a traitor for my uncle. I had to blend in and find a guide with underground dealings." Underground diggers searched and gathered toxic products to sell to weaponize designers. They were extremely secretive and dangerous to contact without a hearsay. "There was a gambler with family ties. All I had to do was have him set the meet up. I didn't know he only speaks for family."

Tariq's hands gripped tightly around the glass. Nearly shattering it. "So, I played a game with him and won." His power swirled and pounded against the room's corners. Ignoring the three of them. "In return he gave me his daughter. As a prize." The hidden rage breaks. Whipping around in a storm of wind. His braids swished and Kai could hear the clink of metal coming from his head. "We honor women. We do not sell, trade, or give women away against their say." Didn't change the fact that it happens. Kai understood, though. He would never sell any woman, especially not from his family. "I gave her honor back by marrying her." Julian coughed out a shocked breath. Kai settled back in his chair. Tariq wasn't done. "The deal was we would divorce when I found the traitor and took him to my uncle, but everything went wrong." He could imagine. It was no different for Rhia and himself, though he was younger than Kai at the time of the incident.

"In the end I was sent back home. The divorce and Aya were forgotten." *No, not forgotten. Pushed back into his farther mind.* If the information was true, it was around three years ago that Tariq took over his uncle's position as head of the family. "When

Aya warned us, I sent scouts to look deeper into her so called to stay in Baton Rouge. She was not stationed in Alexandria. She's living here in Baton Rouge." And if anyone ever learned about her true identity, she would become a target. "She's raising Amon. My uncle's son. Her god-sister's child. She's walking down the damn streets playing mamma." Therefore, already making ties in the House of Alexander.

Julian tapped his sharp nails against the table. "No other choice. To protect her, the child, and yourself, you must completely bring them into the fold. Anyone can hit them. They make you vulnerable." Julian left it unspoken, but the truth was that it would make all of them vulnerable.

"I can't." The whisper told it all. This was what was behind the burning rage and the loss of control. "Estelle, his real mother, she got full custody. The hell if I know how, but she got it. And I swore an oath to my uncle. I will lay no hand upon her. And so long as she breathes, I will not take Amon from her." And it burned Tariq's guts that he had to keep that promise. Julian got a scheming look in his eyes. Kai had a feeling that Estelle wouldn't be a problem for Tariq for much longer. Without him needing to say so, he picked up the jar of burnt ice and quickly poured Tariq a glass.

"Push that to side until the next meet. What shall we do to Rosadina?" In that, they were in agreement. As much as they said they controlled their own fate, they didn't. Neptune's Reading had shown them time and time again that they didn't. And Rhia's... said she ended the Empress. So, he could only thwart Adriana, Rosadina, whomever she wished to be called. They could plan. They could attack, but if destiny had her way, they may not have been able to kill Adriana. There was a ninety percent chance of her surviving if Rhia didn't lay the final strike.

"She laid her trap, I say we use it." The cold distance that had stood between Rhia and him had given him time to plan. None of the movements would work. Adriana was too centered. She would see through every scenario before making a decision. However, using her own methods against her was different. She would never think there was anything wrong with that.

"What do you mean?" Suspension edged Tariq's tone.

"Adriana thinks she seduced me. If I call her up and invite her to a hotel room, she won't believe it's an ambush. She'll come right into our hands." *And tell Rhia.* For days he wondered why she really came to Rhia after so many years. Power. Adriana wanted Rhia's power and to break them. Adriana wanted Rhia in her grasp, and he would use every ounce of his will to stop her.

"Twist it in our favor." Julian's smirk was wide enough to be a smile. *Never seen the man smile.* "I say go for it. Anything you need let me know." And on the desk, he layed down a Colt that Kai had never seen leave Julian's side. Tariq dug within his braids and pulled out a spiral. A circled spike that when activated continuously would circle the room until the safe word is said. Commanded by the owner to hit certain targets. Although Kai had never seen it, he had heard about it plenty enough to know it never left Tariq's head unless he was out of other options. This was their way of showing support. Of being a united front in the alliance. Grasping the weapons in his hands, Kai gave honor to them.

"I bind this between us, what is yours to protect I shall protect. What blood you shall spill you may call upon me and I will answer. As I say I will unto you, you will do for me. Agreed?"

"Agreed," Julian clearly stated.

"Agreed," Tariq clearly said, even as his concentration was

moved to other places. To his woman. The plan had been spoken – now they only had to act on it.

Blackstone Manor
1.14 PM

"Who sent this?" Anger was laced in Rhia's words. The letter crumpled in her hands.
Meet me at Docking Point C for your papers at 4.00.
– A

She knew who it was from. Adriana. Adriana sent it knowing Rhia only wanted Scorpion to contact her. Yet Adriana did and no messenger would hand this to Paul, Kai's bodyguard, to give to her.

"Priscilla handed it to me instead of Sean. You know with the whole messenger thing and all." With the ranks created this way, Paul had become Kai's messenger between the alliance accords. He was Kai's ears, eyes, and a third protection if they should need it. How did Priscilla know that, though? The ranks were only known to members of the organization. "She said the scary lady gave it to her. At her house." Those words could only mean one thing. They had a spy. Not many knew the new address. Along with Priscilla, they kept it secret. Guards were told to pick her up at a near spot with a written note.

"Thank you, Paul." She dismissed him. Kai kept saying she wasn't ready for the truth, and she was tired of being in the dark. She should settle things between her and Adriana. Looking up, she saw that Paul was still there. "What is it, Paul?" The man was waiting for a reason.

"Whatever you do, tell Kai. Don't go running on your own." Paul was a solid rock like Alek. They didn't speak, but they were very protective.

"I won't go alone." It was a good thing he didn't properly listen. She called for Alek. Alessandra would have to wait behind with the car in case they needed her. Doubtful they would, but they shouldn't have thrown caution to the winds.

Docking Point C
4.02 PM

The docking points were once bridges that left the Dust Fields into New Centric. Thirty-seven years ago, it broke down from Radial Waves blast. No one knew where the water came from. It was fresh and healthy. So, the Blackstones decreed that planks would be put down. It was a quiet place for a secret meet. Adriana was standing at the edge of the planks, just a few inches away from the newest formed river. The wind blew her mixed brown and black strands of hair. A tight red coat with a black belt. Short, black ankle boots and white wide pants were what Rhia saw. Alek followed close behind as she stopped a few feet from Adriana. "Where are my papers?" Adriana dug into her coat and pulled out a large envelope, but she didn't hand it to Rhia.

"When we were young you were so quiet. And shy. You stayed in the kitchen. I didn't even know Scorpion was training you until a year before we broke out." Memory Lane? Like seriously! "You always liked secrets and puzzles. You could figure a person out in seconds." The cold front hit them from the left. She blew warm air on her hands and touched them to her face.

"Your point?" she asked as the cold begins to seep into her bones. It was windy enough to give a hard chill. She was hungry again. She had a headache. And the morning sickness was no joke. She just wanted to get her papers, get a clue on the spy, go home and plan her next action.

"My point is why you never figured out mine?" She was confused. *Adriana's secret?* "About whom and what exactly I was." Before Rhia's eyes, Adriana's mixed brown and black strands changed to blood red with white edges and shortened to her neck. Her light eyes changed from blue to pitch black. Her cheekbones become higher. Her eyebrows narrowed down. Her skin lightened and became very pale. A Physiochanger. Able to shape and change their form of any gender and part of their body. Before the Campris Wars, they were born with both genitals. Radiation and everything changed that. Pitch-black eyes. Pale skin. Blood Red hair. Rosadina. And when Adriana smiled, she never saw the attack. She didn't even remember being knocked out. She walked straight into Adriana's ambush.

Taken

Song Dedication: That's my Girl by Fifth Harmony

It was pure shock to see it. The change. How she became slender and taller. Pale skin. White frosted lips. Blood red hair. Pitch-black eyes as dark as night. Rosadina. Adrenaline burst inside Alek and he was moving. A dark shadow appeared before him. "They need to talk. Don't interfere." Light brown hair, dark black eyes, his height nearly matched Alek's, but his eyes picked up and compared their muscle mass. Alek had more, so he body slammed all his muscles into a powerful force, colliding with the man's upper chest. He was aiming for an upper lift and slam dropped on his back. He was gone before Alek could turn things in his favor. Confused, he turned his back to Rhia. It was just a second. He shimmered in before Alek in a dark cloud. "It is not a fight. It is only a talk. Stand down before I put you down."

"I only take orders from my *Dona*." As he was talking, Alek was making a move for his final card. Shadow marks. Those whose legacies were forever changed during the Campris Wars. Their looks and the power that they were now born with. Nearly eighty percent made up the broken territories of the United States. Only ten percent of them were more of a weapon than a power... It was the same for himself. Unlike others who delighted in the show of their power, Alek had kept his hidden. A secret to be used when the best advantages were needed. He bundled the sound against his chest. Building it until the breath in his body was nearly gone. Then releasing it with a wail. As the sound waves rebounded against the planks and river, the man simply vanished in the mist of darkness.

"You're Rosadina." The truth was more painful than it should have been considering the circumstances. The lies. Rhia meant Adriana had touched something that did not belong to her. She had almost killed Adriana and it left her slightly troubled since. Yet, Adriana was…

"Surprised. I guess he didn't tell you after all." Adriana pulled at the thick black gloves she had on. "When Roland told me that Malachi played me…" Her eyes creased in hate. "I thought it was a lie. Just look at me. I'm gorgeous. Men fall under my feet. It's just that I have no desire for men. So, Kai seemed so easy. He wasn't." As she spoke, Rhia saw the scene of that day more clearly. Kai wasn't pushing her away, but he also wasn't pulling her close. And the relief on his face. How did Rhia miss that at the time? "Today he sent a note to my hotel room. The one I thought he arranged because he just couldn't let me go. Hmph! What foolishness? Of course, I used the room." Rhia heard the snick of a lock being open. "He thinks I'll fall into his ambush. Instead, I created this. After all you no longer trusted him enough to come together and his note ensured that he wasn't home. In other words, you're alone." And the smile she sent Rhia's way chilled her bones and froze her body. Then Adriana sent up a flare with blinding light. A signal.

Kai told them that she would be meeting him at a hotel. He didn't mention that he already had her set up in one. It slipped his mind at the moment. Why would it matter? It would only make things easier for them. However, when he arrived, walking inside the room, he could tell that no one had been there for quite a while. The bed was made. The curtains were closed. There wasn't a speck of a scent of food or perfume. Adriana hasn't been in this room for hours. There was a small envelope on the bed. His name was written in elegant cursive writing.

Lose Something? – Rosadina Volvikov

On instinct, he sought out the bond between Rhia and him.

Rhia. The tingles sprung through his mind, bursting with the startling color of life.

Kai. Barely there. Surrounding the sound with worry, loss, and despair.

Where are you? He could feel the adrenaline surge through her body. Pumping with raging fear. Her heart bounced against her chest like a hammer.

I... love you. In a splash of smoke, the bond was cut off from her end. Ice raced through his veins and he poured the coldness into more welcoming emotions like determination. His beast. His dragon. Jazier spun and circled his body.

"Find her. Kill any who get in your way." His ice-blue eyes glowed with dark intensity. "Go." Jazier had a need to find her as much as he did. His tail lashed against Kai in anger as he flew away.

Anya. Her spirit stood next to him. Breathing against his back. He could feel her fury bath behind his neck. "Search all of Louisiana. Give me the name of every person involve in her abduction. I'll have their heads." The promise satisfied her on a smaller scale. With the snap of her fingers, she blinked out of his sight. Traveling over thousands of miles. Covering every inch in her maddening search. Storming out the hotel, he commanded Sean to contact Paul. Enough of dodging bullets. When he got Rhia back, Rosadina would die.

Rescue

Song Dedication: Somebody Help Me by Full Blown Rose

5.17 PM

She came through with a throbbing headache. Shadows swished before her eyes in dim colors. "What did the Blackstone *Don* see in her? Chick has no figure." The squeak of a voice behind her reached her ears.

"I'd fuck her in a minute. Figure or not." That hacker-chocked voice like someone who had been practically smoking since their teen years.

"The Empress would kill ya. You ain't hear it fer me, but she be saying tis here her treasure. She'd cut ye in half." The southern drawl with country twang was higher than the other voices.

"Well, damn." The hacker coughed between his words. She could feel the roaming of his eyes. Slick and sick as he gazed over her body. It burnt up her back and threw her into an old nightmare. He had the same feel of the Jang brothers. It disgusted her and makes her scared. She didn't know what would happen to the baby if he tried to act on his own idea. A chained door slammed in front of her. The light gave her a chance to see her surroundings. Bodies. Hundreds of bodies. Packed on top of each other against the far back square wall. Old black large lockers on each side. Swinging small bulbs of light. Dingy. Spotted brown floor. A strong scent of dirt, blood, and dried mud. In walked a demon in a dress. An even worse nightmare than the ones from her childhood. The men behind her jumped to their feet.

"Empress." Their three voices rang loudly out of tune with respect.

"Leave us," Adriana commanded and so now they were alone. Her sister. Her enemy. "I really had hoped it wouldn't come to this. I wanted you to join us, but you didn't leave him." She frowned in despair. True despair. As if Kai and Rhia breaking up would have been her happiest moment.

"Anyone ever tell you that expectations are meant to be broken?" Hate was clearly heard along with her words. Adriana's hands balled into a fist. Her eyebrows burrowed further down between her eyes. The pitch-black darkened even more than Rhia believed it could. Like a black abyss, they latched onto and dared not move away from Rhia's center. Adriana stepped quick, her hand raised, and Rhia tugged on her powers. Only to get not a spark of it. It was gone. Wrong. Blocked. And she was as defenseless as a babe. It was just like the orphanage. She could only close her eyes and grit her teeth against the pain. Except it never came. She could suddenly feel cold fury surrounding her body. As she opened her eyes, she came back to face Kai's Dragon.

"Jazier," she whispered.

"Impossible." Fear shattered the simmered silence. "I put a shield on you. You should not be able to call upon your powers." A shield. Only a dark priest or priestess could break the damn thing. Jazier wasn't hers, though. He belonged solely to Kai. Jazier faced Adriana with his sharp fangs pronged outward. A roar, breathing down with cold frosted smoke escaped his nostrils. His claws snicked and clicked against the dusted ground. "How is he here?" The demand was nearly screamed at her. She could taste Adriana's fear. Things weren't going the way Adriana planned, and for once that scared her.

"He's here because he's not mine." Rhia said it slowly. Taunting the fact that Adriana had miscalculated.

"This is Kai? He's a Shadow Marked?" With Jazier keeping her in a protective circle, Rhia knew it was only a short time before Kai found her.

"You're a dead woman, Adriana. A Tamer has you in sight."

Docking Point C
5.17 PM

Scorpion's heart slammed into his chest, waking him from near death. He gasped, sucking in a large breath to fill his lungs. Rolling to his side, he saw the disaster of the docking point. He should have known. Adriana could make many a men tremble to their knees, but she never could stand to be used. Going to his knees, he glanced around for Hummingbird. He saw her bodyguard. The damn Boomer. If it was a second more, he would have gotten the full force of his second wave. And that idiot Adriana just had to get one more attack before going back home. "Hummingbird." The dust caused him to have a coughing fit. Staggering to her guard, he was on the ground with multiple lacerations. He was dying. "If I save you, there will be consequences. You and yours will be bound and loyal to me." Alek's will told Scorpion that he wished to live, so Scorpion figured he would be useful in the future.

"Er gi les ton, *Dona*." The odd foreign language rose on the wind of settled destruction. Even though he had never heard the language, he immediately understood what the guard was saying.

Loyalty only to my *Dona*. Even upon death… Scorpion slashed a small blade against his wrist. The blood dripped onto the guard's lips.

"Drink, they call me Death's Raider." A Raider was known to command the living and had control over the dead. Some able to heal to anyone and bring those at death's door back to life. Some could command a life to be taken. A death's raider could do both. As if striving away from a quaking thirst, he drank.

"En tol ka jai sei." They took her. Rage pounced like a tiger in him. Damnation Adriana. Just as the guard fell under a short sleep of his healing power, a woman and Malachi came running up to him. *Heavenly High Lord above. What now?*

5.22 PM

Kai saw him and red coated his eyes. The bastard. Alessandra ran over to check on Alek. "I really should kill you," he said as his men surrounded the mystery man. However, Kai wouldn't, as he may have had information that Kai wanted.

"Not as much as I wish to kill you. Heavenly High Lord mate why'd ye let her come with just da one guard. Adriana though it may not seem is impulsive." His words enraged Kai.

"And who was it that lured her here?" Grasping at the flaps of his coat, Kai wished to knock him unconscious.

"Not I. Rhia asked for help to disappear. We only got da paper fer her. It be ye doing that has her a running." Running? What for? There had been no sign that Rhia wanted to leave. She was angry, but not enough to walk.

"She's pregnant." Those gasping words came from Alek as Alessandra helped him to stand. "She didn't want you to know."

Kai closed his eyes and breathed deeply. When he opened them, they collided with that infuriating man. His enemy, but also his ally.

"So be it. Gather our people. We're getting my family back." Brennan and Sean fell back to act on his orders.

"You be going to rescue her?" mystery man asked. Kai didn't know his exact relationship with Rhia, but he could guess. Mari was a younger sister of her heart from the orphanage. And she had stayed with Adriana. Therefore, this man must also be a sibling from the orphanage. Unlike Adriana, he seemed to want her safe.

"You may join us." And Kai turned his back to him. His only responsibility now was to get Rhia and their child back home safely.

Death's Legacy

Song Dedication: Rise by Katy Perry

7.15 PM

Can you still not break free? Jazier questioned, even though his voice was ringing in her mind much too loudly. The distance from Kai meant that communication had to be on his natural pathway. For hours, she had struggled to break the shield wrapped around her wrist.

"It isn't any good, Jazier. I'm not a dark priestess." She had struggled for hours without hope.

I cannot contact Malachi. And the radiation here is harmful to the cub. She never felt the need to be rescued as much as today. That was how she learned that you do and say foolish things when the time becomes dark. In what seemed like the end of all, she had told Jazier about the baby. *You must continue to try for him. For your cub.* Frustrated with his constant insistence that she continue to fight against a binding that she was incapable of breaking, she glared harshly up at him. Only to freeze. The lockers were gone. Instead, a man chained inside of a dark cage faced her. He was resting with his eyes closed. Not peacefully. She could see the bright sharp points of… fangs. Triangular and two inches long. Dark, tan skin. Deep, long, blue-black inked markings on his shoulders, chest, and she could see on the small tip coming from his back. Long, thin legs. Small shoulders.

Lanky and fragile he looked, yet the pure wild purple aura showed his glorious strength. This was not someone easily defeated.

"Do you see him?" she asked Jazier, for if she was hallucinating then there was no need to save her. For she was already lost.

He is well hidden. I am surprised that even a True Seer such as yourself can see him, he stated as if a man she could not hours ago see but could now do so was normal. As she stared at the dark and beautiful man, something awoke in her. As if he and she were the same. Consumed by what that could mean, his eyes opened, and she stared into her own. One hunter-green and one a deep purple. Odd and yet enchanting.

Deseark. Descendent. The words enacted her fate.

Atlantis Sky
7.17 PM

When her eyes collided with his own, Althea felt the weight of more than a thousand years of loneliness lift from her shoulders. His alluring eyes glowed like bright orbs at Rhia. "Deseark." Descendant. Through Rhia, she could hear the straining whisper of his voice. He recognized Rhia. He knew in Rhia's veins flowed the blood of two of them.

"Vikhtor." Anguish and longing poured from her like the hard fall of rain. Free him, she wished to command, but she could not. She couldn't force fate even though Althea was the named Goddess of Fate. However, she could do one thing. "Daerhae, bring me Rhia's string." Standing beside her and staring into the whirling pools of present events, Daerhae turned until her gaze was burning into Althea's very being. "What is it?" It was a terse question. Stiff in her demand. The fact that Daerhae had denied her.

"Can we not wait? She is pregnant. It could be harmful." Yes, it could. It would not be.

"Bring me Rhia's string." No longer defiant, Daerhae went to the cabinet. People used to talk about the three fates. That they controlled every human's fate, and they could end it at any moment. That was far from the truth. As her husband had called her, Althea only could define the fates of the Deseark. The descendants of Gods and Goddesses. Rhia's string was the rare twisted colors of gold and white. Unlike the ones before her legacy, Rhia was born with the ability to become a demigoddess. If Althea so wished. Daerhae brought her the string. Almost sensing what it was she was planning to do to it, the string begin to brighten with a colossal range of interchangeable colors. Deciding what it would become? Taking the old sheers, she slashed against the string. Then quickly she tied it, binding it once again. In bated breath she watched and waited. It lengthened in three score lengths and changed from two solid separate colors of white and gold into three intertwining twist colors of black, green, and ocean blue. And it was no longer just Rhia's string. It was the string of her Hunter's Clan. What would be done to Rhia so would be done to all who belonged to her.

Blackstone Manor
7.19 PM

Jazier hadn't returned since Kai commanded that he found Rhia. It worried him. It should not have taken Jazier this long to find someone whose essence that he had looked into. Soon the sun would begin setting. They had to find her while the light was still burning. Anya swept around like the little fairy she looked like. "Did you find her?" She shook her head no. Her tiny eyes were downcast. Her pale gray skin became a dark black in worry.

"Someone's blocked off the huntress in her. I've tried just about everything, Rahl Malachi. I've no hope of finding a huntress without any power to call." Desolate. He stared at the map on his desk. According to Roland, they didn't come in an autodrive. They walked, but that didn't mean Adriana didn't have transportation on standby. So, the next question in point was if this a quick grab. If so, just how far did she get?

"I hear that you're going to be a Dad?" Julian came up behind him, his dagger tipping around the map.

"Hmm." Maybe she was still in the Dust Fields area.

"Tamers are a lot like Sifters. They have dual instincts." His chatter annoyed Kai, but the man hadn't said anything without thought yet. "More so than Sifters their blood ties are stronger. For they could use their animal's senses to find their mate and children." He dragged the dagger back into his jacket pocket and leaves. Memories surfaced from long ago. Kai's mother had gone missing and his father sat down to meditate. Quietly he watched as it seemed his very essence disappeared before Kai's eyes. When he stood up, he took Kai along on a rescue. Some low-level street drug lords had taken her and he knew exactly where she was. She was six months pregnant with Lucy. His animal. His dragon. Jazier. Taking that into account, he sat down behind his desk. Then he meditated until he could feel himself separating from his body. In an instant, he was standing beside Jazier and Rhia. She was watching with fascinating awe as a strange man knelt before her, breaking the bonds of a shield. Taking a quick glance around, Kai recognized exactly where she was. The frontal warehouse at Docking Point A. His spirit slammed back into his body.

He found Tariq and Julian facing him with grim determination. "You knew?" If he were to guess, he had just astral walked, meaning he wouldn't have been breathing and his heart would seem to have stopped temporarily.

"I researched. There was a 93.4 percent of chance." Julian smirked as if he never doubted his calculations.

"She's still at the Docks. Let's go." There was much to this world. Life. Death. Powers of irrational kind, but love he guessed would always be the same. For everyone would fight for love if nothing else.

7.16 PM

The man had broken from the chains, his eyes never leaving her. He walked with gray smoke hovering around him. "You are my Deseark. Blood of my blood." Thin-chained veins crossed his throat as he spoke. Disappearing when he did not. His words sounded odd and coarse against his sharpened teeth. "I am Vikhtor. Your ancestor. God of Death, Vengeance, and Judgement." She watched as he named himself – the ink moved to pictorial snapshots. A wide, thin hooked knife that spoke of death. Flaming blood dropped in a ball that screamed vengeance. And the slamming of a mantle that would hit in small pecks that she knew he could feel it. There was a perceptible flinch each time it came down. "I can free you, but at a price." Just as she was about to accept any price that he could demand, she recalled where she had heard the name before. Vikhtor. Neptune's

Reading.

"I was supposed to free you." Yet he didn't look like he needed her help.

"You are not yet ready to free me." He turned just enough for her to see the truth. His body was still bound in chains. His eyes closed in true peace. "I am only a projection..." That knowledge pained him. It pained her. Her very being was being drawn to him. Still, he was right. She could feel the fact that she wasn't strong enough to help him become fully free.

"I'm sorry." She really was. Now that she saw him, she wanted more than ever to help him, and she couldn't.

"Don't be. If I set you free you must promise to act as me." She had no idea what acting as him would entail, but she knew it was important. If that was the only thing she could do for him, then so be it.

"Yes." With her acceptance, she could feel the burn on her neck, back, and right arm. She saw a replica of the hooked knife on her arm. It was in stasis.

"You are my heir. My legacy." And then he bent down and broke the bond of a shield. Freeing her. He vanished in a quick blow of smoke.

We must go. Jazier flew around her in a protective circle as they moved to the door. They had left Rhia alone after Empress exited. Not Adriana, her sister. Not even Rosadina. They called her Empress with coveting lust. Until she killed Empress, that was what Rhia would address her as. The door opened before Rhia could get to it.

"Why couldn't you be more like your mother-in-law. Why in the hell must you always fight? Geneva welcomed her death." Empress's minions poured in and pushed her back. She payed them no mind because she was mentally analyzing Empress' words and coming to a shaking conclusion.

"You killed *Madre*?" Empress laughed lightly, but didn't get too close to Rhia. Of course not, a few of her men hadn't done so well in that aspect while Rhia was mentally checked out. By their appearance and the sounds of painful groans, Jazier had handled it perfectly.

"I can have an incestuous relationship with Maya. Why can I not murder my weak and loving aunt? She was your mother-in-law, not your mother." Rhia's sight was blinded by a darkening onyx. A furious beast rose in her and took over. She was hungry. Her thirst only to be abated by blood and death.

Tears of the Loss

Song Dedication: Somebody to Die For by Hurts

7.32 PM

Dina saw death. Since she decided to go along with the idea of taking back the United State Territories, she knew it to be a long battle. A fight day after day for many years to come. Even though Sovereign wasn't shadow-marked, she was not afraid. Of anything. For her plan was so perfect that there was no doubt of their success. Dina had forgotten that there could be a catalyst. Something so small that could erupt and blow the lands to hands of grain. A catalyst that could happen anywhere at any time. It could be anything or anyone. From the first day of the attack, Rhia had been her catalyst. As she transformed before Dina, she realized her mistake. Taunting Rhia. Taking Rhia. Trying to trick and bind Rhia to her will. It had all come down to this moment. Rhia's hair grew until it reached her ankles. It lightened until it became a light cool blue with platinum tipped edges. Her eyes glowed with frightening brightness. It shone with the clear beauty of the moon's luminescent light. And her tan skin darkened until it matched the night sky. She grew sharp, short, curved claws and she roared with the deep echo of vengeance. Dina stood, quaking in her clothes. Afraid for the first time that she might not survive. Rhia was *her* death.

7.33 PM

The wind was circling. Swirling in a cyclone move they slowly descended over docks. "Storm's coming. It'll hit under half an hour. We won't want to be here at that time." Roland spoke to infuriate Kai. He knew it. The storm reminded him of where this all began. That day he visited Colt Engineering, they got the wind and humid air from the Irene hurricane that swept up Florida. Back then, *Madre* had activated protocol and contacts were called up for the check points. That's when word reached them that trouble was in Baton Rouge. A few days later he met Rhia. She saved his life. He forced her to marry him. That day was so long ago he had forgotten what Rhia once reminded him. Rhia was a storm. Powerful. Passionate. Thrilling. Dangerous. A fury raging nature. And now… a new storm brewed. Dark gray clouds. The sound of a thunderclap. Clashing of lightning bolts. Here he stood, making a new path for them as he set about to rescue Rhia.

"Make it quick and efficient. Take down any man in the way." He had a small group. Sean, Paul, Brennan, Roland, Julian and Tariq. However, Rosadina, according to Roland, had ninety-seven percent of men who were not shadow marked. The other three percent had sworn a binding oath to be loyal only to him. Rosadina couldn't command them. Of his small group, there was not a man who was not shadow marked. "Don't dally. If you find Rhia, send up the flare and get out." As they moved, a wailing siren hit the docks, and the river waves crashed over. They rushed inside as the water collapsed on the walking planks. Breaking them and pulling them in. The cyclone dropped into the river. Bombing the water. The water rose, surfacing to the sky in a dense compound of colors. Fire gold red orange, the deep abyss black, dark pure hunter green, deep purple, and crashing sea blue. The bond between Rhia and him clawed open with tearing strikes. Strips of his soul peeled off and he found himself facing a being that he knew was Rhia. Long, pale, blue hair swishing about her like the awakening sea storm. Dark, black skin that glistened in the day. And her eyes that glowed and pulled him like a siren's song. Shining with a sadness so strong it nearly brought him to tears. And a fury so bold it burned his insides to ashes.

"Dear Heavens, Althea has made her a demigoddess," Anya whispered. Her fear shook her tiny form till she zoomed in and out like a hummingbird.

"Like the myths?" Before the question was finished, Anya was already shaking her head.

"The myths you know are far from the truth. Rahl Malachi if you don't get to Rhia soon, the Louisiana territories will cease to exist." He watched the truth before his eyes. The cyclone was now pulling up the edge of the docking points. Swallowing up the stalling cycles.

"Run," he commanded. He took a turn following the tightly bound thread within his spirit. Praying to the Mother of the Sky that he had made it to Rhia before she caused a catastrophe.

Acid dripped from Rhia's claws. Burning with the intent to kill and maim. The Empress' guards boxed her in. Attempting to keep Rhia away. She easily flipped them over out of her way. One brave and foolish soul ran to her as a distraction. Her claws caught him up, slamming into his stomach and ripping his intestines from his body. The acid melted them into pools of black goo. He was dead before he dropped to the floor. Shocked, they didn't move for a second, just staring down at the bloody mass of death. "What the hell do you think you're doing? Defend me." The Empress squawked like a startled crow. Azai, long swords, short swords, daggers, exploding pints. They had it all. It wouldn't do them any good.

"Jazier, only one." He may play with only one of them. The rest were hers. Including the Empress. Adrenaline pumped into her veins. Throbbing inside her bloodstream. She didn't think. She didn't see. She could only feel and know. Flexing all her muscles, she flew. As she danced around her opponents in quick, unseen movements, her claws dug into bodies, tearing through organs and crushing hearts. She cracked open skulls and slashed at meat, ripping lines of skin by the tendons. The cries of pain were enchanting music to her ears. She bathed in the splattered blood as if given a spring of rain. In the end, no man was left standing, and she had lost the Empress. "Malachi is here. We need to go." Like Jazier, she knew the moment Kai stepped onto the ground that he was close. His shoulder slouched down even more as he walked near her. Being away from Kai had nearly depleted his energy and strength. He couldn't stay by her side and keep up the fight. "You go – there is more blood for me to spill." His scales shimmered into a colder blue than before. Angry at her defiance, but understanding her thirst for vengeance, he blew tiny ice shards at her. A peck against her skin.

Be quick, he commanded. More and more she saw his master in him.

"Always," she promised. Jazier's tail whipped behind her head as he flew away. Purposely giving her a gentle pat on her head. Following the trail of Kai's essence. And she obtained a big gulf of air. Scenting for Empress. Her eyes slit into cat eyes and everything became two-sided. The physical form of the warehouse and her true sight showed her their hidden auras. The

Empress was a blob of depressed gray and chalky white.

Kai was right in the eye of the storm. The floorboards quivered and crack beneath his feet, making his steps unsteady. The wind howled behind his ears blocking all sounds. Glass from the old tile windows crashed inward as he moved forward. His men were scattered. Death was an awful taste amidst the air. He came face to snout with Jazier, but no Rhia. "Where is she?"

She went after Rosadina. There was no question of what going after Rosadina meant.

"We ride." Jazier lowered until he touched the ground. Kai kicked over him and riding straps appeared in his hand. Gripping them tight, he connected the Huntzguard bond to Jazier so that he could find Rhia faster. She was outside in the back just behind the storm. There wasn't much time. Fighting against the raging wind, they raced to her. High above them, he could see her facing off Rosadina. The demigoddess and the mortal. Claws against short swords. Rhia's powers were bursting within her. Pounding more and more as the hunt awakened in her. Blinding her to all of her but her surroundings. The cyclone was blackening. Becoming as near black as her skin. More than a third of the warehouse had been sucked into the vortex. Just over the other side men fought with the fear of the last day. Vigilantly willing their strength so that they may live another day. He knew if he didn't find a way in exactly one minute then they were over. The vortex would swallow all of the people and territories of Louisiana. "Do you fear death?" he asked Jazier as he watched a man behind Rhia raise his gun shakenly. Aiming at her. She was too distracted to sense him.

I fear weakness.

That's good. As Rhia's anchor, he was the only one that

could pull her back from the destructive power. At all cost.

"Today we die." He pushed all of his weight into Jazier and they descended. Falling, memories of these last few months flowed through his mind. Meeting Rhia. Commanding her. That bold woman in the red dress hiding the child as she walked into his club. Red Wing as she showed why she deserved the name *Dona*. The first time they made love. Her smile. Her laugh. Her despair at *Madre's* death. Her eyes as they flashed with intense anger. Everything about her was beautiful. Everything that made Rhia who she was, that was why he came to love her. The pow of the gun blazes at a distance. If he was lucky, it was a capsule, which meant a quick death. If he wasn't, then it was a bullet. It crashed just two inches from his heart. He wasn't lucky. Jazier rolled along with him.

"Kai!" Rhia screamed. She abandoned her battle and came running. The patter of her running feet were so loud and distance. She was kneeling over him. Big pools of tears filled her eyes as they dropped from her face. "Kai," she called to him softly.

"De wei a y mo." *With love may we meet in the sunrise again.* They tugged against his lips as he handed the prayer back to her, for them to meet in a second life.

"No," she demanded. "No," she commanded. His heart beat slushed as his heart rate slowed. Blood poured from him. Her hands pressed against the wounds. He saw her hair change from the pale ocean blue to its natural blue-black. It shortened and curled, big and wild. The way that he loved it. "I'm pregnant. You better not have me raising this child by myself." Even as she said this, the tears wouldn't end because she knew the truth. Her caramel cocoa skin sparkled in the sunset.

Jazier, take care of her. And he closed his eyes for the last time, leaving Jazier to protect her always.

Ties of the Bonded

Song Dedication: Living on a Highwire by Lemonade Mouth

7.58 PM
Docking Warehouse

Jazier, take care of her. His last words echoed in her mind. Some twisted thread tied a communication between them still. She could hear what he said to Jazier. She could feel what his moments were like. A sense of hopelessness. Yet no pain. He was already floating away from her.

"Nooo." The scream escaped from her with a loud explosion. Did it make sense that his death brought night life? Did it make sense that his death stopped the storm? Did it make sense that his death ended the battle and destruction even though the Empress had escaped? No, it didn't. That bullet was meant for her. It hit him, but it punched through her soul. The scuffle and scrap of his fall was her being torn open. The slow beat of his heart as the bullet went through a vital artery. His death was hers. His last breath was her. His last memories were her. And the truth was heartbreaking. Anguish choked her throat, blocking away her breath. Ashes of burned wood drifted to the earth like snowflakes.

"He's gone, *Dona*. We have to go." That was Sean talking to her. His voice gentle, soft, and filled with as much grief as herself.

"I can't." *He's alone. He's not supposed to leave by himself.* "I can't." The pain ached inside her entire being. Sean helped her take her hands from him. The blood stains in evidence. Her eyes couldn't leave his body. If not for the body and blood, she would think that he was asleep. Resting from a tired day and waiting for them to go home. Together. Tears blinded her sight. *Oh, Mother!*

"You can. You must. For the baby." But she couldn't. So little time they had and it was over. She'd never get that same protection and care. No one else could love her like him. And she could never love another man like him. Realization dawned upon her.

"I didn't get to tell him." They watched her as cold seeped into her veins, numbing all her emotions.

"What didn't you tell him, *Dona*?" *Dona* to remind again of her responsibilities. If her husband was dead, did that still make her a *Dona*? It did not.

"I didn't tell him how I felt." Sean sighed and asked for a coat. She was shaking. Large shakes as she rocked back and forth on her knees. Sean placed the coat around her. It had Kai's scent on it. Oakwood, burning fire, and magnolias. An odd and unique scent that always suited him.

"Then tell him and let's lay him to rest." They faced the opposite way. To give her this moment. She cradled his head in her lap.

"Wu shi er tao. Min quay e las. De wei a y mo." *I love you. My heart goes with you. With love may we meet in sunrise again.* Then she lay a kiss upon his lips. His temperature was already cooling. Her teared fell onto his face. With all that she was, she wished that she could hold onto him and never let go. With shaky legs and a sorrow-filled heart she walked away. Every step heavier than the one before. She couldn't turn back. She needed only go forward. Jazier waited patiently for her. Sean escorted her under his careful watch. He left Paul and Brennan to handle Kai. They would bring him home. To honor him. *Don* Malachi Jonah Blackstone Volvikov. He passed away as a leader and soldier. She sent one last prayer. *Heavenly Mother of the Sky, please bring him back to me one day.*

8.06 PM

Death was not what Kai expected. Maybe because they now knew they had three lives that they had no regrets until the last one. He didn't remember much of his death. How did he die? Why did he die? Standing on a gray path, he only knew that he was dead. There was gray all around. Gray walls, gray room, gray mist. And he was alone. There wasn't a voice anywhere to be heard. Must he wait to pass on? He pondered. Time seemed suspended. Hanging over him. Watching him. Judging. Then a white door appeared next to him. In stepped two people he never thought to see again. "*Madre*. Father." Neither had changed much. Father was seven feet tall, slim, large shoulders, grass-green eyes, chestnut hair with the traditional red edges all pooled back into a ponytail. He was wearing jeans and a shirt. His father never favored new world clothes. *Madre's* hair was cut and she had styled it in lifted spikes. She had on red lipstick, red eyeshadow. She was extremely tiny standing next to his father at five feet in a red, low-cut, V-neck dress. They were smiling at him. They were happy. *Madre* walked up and stood on her tip toes to give him a hug.

"My son." Father took his hand in a warrior's grasp, hands touching just an inch under the inner elbow. The other hand held back of his elbow. Facing his parents after death was peaceful. Until his *Madre* spoke.

"You're not supposed to be here, *Niño*."

"No one can control death. It comes when it wishes." His father eyes scrunched in confusion.

"*Nino*, you're on the gray path." He said it as if that was to mean something to him. Only he didn't know what. "Something's not right. How exactly did you... die, Kai?" His soft tones became loud and defensive.

"I don't remember." Which was the entire truth, however as others could only remember certain things from their past lives, he thought this was normal.

"Mother of the sky." *Madre* gasped in shock. Shaken. Then she pulled herself together. "The gray path is for those not yet fully dead. Their soul is still attached to their body. Only the essence comes here." Hope filled him.

"I can go back?" The answer resonated in him like fireworks going off.

"Yes. Send my love to the girls." Of course, he would. *Rhia, Heavenly Mother, I can go home.*

"When?"

"Now," a voice said, and he woke to the brown leaves, freezing wet grass while flakes of ash snow fell from his body.

8.39 PM

She was cradling his pillow in her arms. She lay on the bed in their room, wishing back to when she would wake to him by her side. There were no more of those days coming. She couldn't contain the tears. Not in the face of Julian and Tariq, though they had to wonder if the alliance was still active. Not in the face of Lucy who had just lost her mother not too long ago. She couldn't watch as Sean and Paul broke the news to the group. She couldn't listen to Alek and Alessandra as they called up other members to give the news of his death. She was the *Dona*, but she was numb. Tired. Her eyes dropped. Blinking. Darkness began to cover as sleeps dragged her in.

Thump.

The small pound of a heart woke her. It was an echo beating near her own rapid heartbeat. A slow beat.

Thump.

Harder against her chest. She heard the quick gasp of breath.

Thump. Thump. Thump.

Faster. Pounding as if to punch out of her chest. Her breath quickened. Her feet moved without her knowledge. She was running. Running out the room. Down the steps. Outside to the far back. By the shack. Running because her heart and instincts told her so. Guards blocked her path. *Move.* She needed them to move. She pushed and pushed and pushed. They were stone walls. "Clear the path," he said. The voice froze her in her frustrating attempt on the guards. There he stood with a blooming new mark. A golden hummingbird with red wings spread wide in majestic manner. On his naked bared chest. The black jeans hug tightly to him even without a belt. Everything slowed down as she caught sight of every inch that made him. Short, black waves with red edges. Soft, chocolate-brown eyes. Small, plump lips. All over six feet tall of her gorgeous man. *Mine.* She ran and wrapped her arms around him. He was real. He was alive. She cradled his jaw, wanting to kiss him. Wanting more proof that he was alive.

"Heavenly Mother of the Sky, thank you." Her prayers were

answered. If another prayer wouldn't come true it did not matter. This was the greatest prayer the Mother had ever answered.

"Welcome back, Rahl Malachi." The chime of Anya's voice broke her reservation.

"You knew?" Just guessing that made her want to rip Anya's head from her body. Not that she could. Anya's physical body was back in the Dust Fields. This was more of a projection of her form that she used for them.

"Yes."

"Why did you not say anything?" Her wings fluttered against the wind, her hands upon her hips.

"You had to live out the lesson. That time is short and life is precious. Enjoy every second of it." Kai's hands wrapped around her waist. He walked them down the path that their organization had created.

"We shall. That we shall."

What It Means to Live

Song Dedication: We Don't Talk Any more, covered by Kurt Hugo Schneider, and Fly by Nicki Minaj, ft. Rihanna

Roland came into her office just as Dina was celebrating her success. Malachi was dead and Rhia was grieving too much to come after her. He stood in the doorway with a smile gracing his face. "Come to celebrate with me traitor." She knew he had to be out of the way when she kidnapped Rhia. She just never expected him to turn his back on her and help Malachi Blackstone in Rhia's rescue. The devil of a man. Where was his loyalty?

"I do hope you are not celebrating Malachi's death." He poured the vintage champagne into the flute of a glass.

"Why ever not?" After all, the first act was complete. When she got rid of Julian Francesco and Tariq Alexander, the Sovereign plan would reach its highest point and she would rule the United Territories as their Sovereign, The Supreme Ruler. She took a sip of her drink.

"He's alive."

And nearly choked upon it.

"How?" Her hands shook as she recalled the events that led to his death. And Rhia… that thing… that she became. She never wished to face that being again.

"That is an answer for the heavens. I only came to say goodbye." Fury burned many people, but fury had always cooled Dina. Gave her a clearer head when needed.

"You leave my side to go fight with her." Of course, she didn't need to say Rhia's name. They both know of whom she spoke of.

"I choose no side. These events have altered my path. I need to channel my spirit to direct me on my next course." He slipped into the shadows, dispersing with the shades of darkness.

"Damn it." Dina slammed the flute under her hands onto her desk. Pain crushed against her palms. Small bits of blood scattered past her fingertips on the desk. The dark red reminded her that if she could not succeed then she would surely die.

Blackstone Manor
Aug 21, 3034
8.37 PM

Malachi decided to host a celebration. In a way, he had many reasons to celebrate even during these times of war. The man came back from the dead. His rescue of Rhia resulted in Rosadina's numbers to dwindle at such a high level that Dina Ignis had to retreat in order to regroup. That gave them a small time of peace. No mysterious questions or identities to figure out. They could all rest thanks to him. Not to mention the baby. He was going to be a father. So yes, the entire Blackstone organization had to know. Almost made Tariq jealous of him. If he did not know the truth behind that happiness. The struggle and fight that brought them to this day.

His communication device beeped inside his pocket. The chatter of other people forces him to answer outside. A man in his early forties appeared on his device. Graysideburns, light black and gray mixed colored braids. Braids that signified that they were still in war. Lower braids told how many lives had been taken by him. Glassy, blue eyes, high cheekbones. Flat, white teeth gritted in anger. Red-brown skin from the war paint hiding their true skin tone.

"You need to come to Olive Street. Aya wants to leave with Amon." Aya, his wife. Amon the son of his uncle and, by clan tradition, his nephew. Aya who he only just learned was Amon's biological mother, godsister, and had been raising him in Baton Rouge for the last three years.

"Scorch me, I'll be there." He maneuvered himself around the crowd until he stood before Kai and his wife Rhia. Rhia was all aglow. She had on a bright yellow Sunday dress that really suited her. Her hair was down, and it framed around her face like gentle moving waves. No makeup. A natural beauty. Kai stood just to her side in a navy-blue, old world shirt and loose, black jeans. More likely to suit her taste. He was talking to his sister who was finally coming back out of her shell. These last few months had hit them the worst. He tapped him on his shoulder to get his attention. "I got to go. Problem with my wife." The words had slipped out before he could bring them back.

"Understand. Hope everything is okay and let me know if you need anything," was all he said. So much had changed in Louisiana because of the war. He never thought he would have an alliance with anyone. Yet he did. His partners were men that he respected. Walking away he had a feeling that it was now his turn to front the battle. For living they can repeat mistakes. They would look upon their regrets. In Tariq's case, Aya was both, and the war had brought her back to him. It wouldn't be easy, but that was what it meant to live.

"He's married?" Rhia was shocked. The alliance tied Julian,

Tariq, and Kai together. However, it was her rescue that brought the three of them closer. Kai was most tight lipped about things that were personal when conversing among themselves. "And you didn't bother to tell me." Even if it was personal, she at least should meet and know his wife. The woman wasn't an outsider in all of this.

"It's his life. He is living that path and we must live our own." Giving him her full attention. Happiness was a ray beam shining around her.

"And how shall we live?" That small and simple smile appeared on his face.

"Together. As lovers. As warriors. As fighters. De wei a y mo. Wu shi er tao." His hand held her own tightly. Their bond was stronger than ever. The words and feelings flowed between them.

"De wei a y mo. Wu shi er tao su." *I love you too.*